# 5TH

# GENDER

# THE
# 5TH
# GENDER

A TINKERED STARS MYSTERY

# G. L. CARRIGER

GAIL CARRIGER LLC

# GAIL CARRIGER, LLC

# THE 1ST CHAPTER

## *What's with the pet thing anyway?*

*There is no doubt about it. Humans are weird.*

Surely all the other aliens would agree with Tristol on this subject – especially at the pub (which was run by humans) on the space station (also run by humans). But humans could be efficient in their weirdness and often quite fun. And no one argued with the fact that they were awfully prolific in all things, breeding faster than any other space-faring species ever encountered in the charted galaxy. They spread. Like fungus. They also spread their legs. *A lot.*

They were cute, though. Tristol admitted that. Fertile sexy brown-toned creatures, humans, with those adorable round little ears and petal shaped eyes.

But they were also *weird.*

Take the whole *keeping of pets* thing. Who would have dreamed up such an eccentricity? Keep an animal in one's abode intended for neither work nor food but just companionship? Very weird.

Tristol, however, was a galoi, the notoriously easygoing *loga* variant, too. Which meant that once he met one of these so-called *pets*, he was rather taken with the concept. Or at least, this particular sample thereof.

*Cat*neuter*pet* Mister Montiguous was currently under Tristol's care. And Tristol was utterly enamored of the funny hairy four-footed beastie. To have charge of a *cat*, particularly *this cat*, was a truly sacred responsibility.

Mister Montiguous's humans were away on their *second honeymoon*. Tris had been chosen to feed the cat, and to pet the cat, and to call the cat a *wonderful feline creature*.

Tristol had no idea what a *second honeymoon* meant. To start with, the word *honeymoon* was mysterious. What did the excrement of bees and a satellite astral body have to do with spousal contracts? And then, why did one need two of them?

*Human*female*friend* Elle spoke eloquently about wanting to *sit on sand and drink fruity drinks with umbrellas in them for her second honeymoon.*

Tristol's hair quivered in confusion. *Why sand? Would not sand get into certain intimate places? Most uncomfortable.* Then, after looking up the word *umbrella* because it was new to him, there being no weather on a space station, Tris was also left wondering, *Why stick a large accessory meant for rain into one's drink? Would this not damage both the accessory and the drink? Seemed a soggy bit of business.*

But Elle and *human*male*friend* Olav (Elle's spousal contract) were excited about the whole endeavor. Since Tris spent most of his life excited about something, he was always delighted to facilitate the sensation in others. So he sent his *human*heterosexual*spousal-unit*friends* off on their weird *soggy*sandy*honey-moon* thingy and undertook the task of looking after their cat.

Mister Montiguous was a diminutive furry creature who happened to miraculously weigh the same as a small asteroid when standing on one's chest. Tris thought dark matter might be involved. The cat had the general attitude that if given due worship, devotees would be rewarded with a loud rumbling sub-vocalization (called *a purr*) and the occasional tiny tongue lick.

Tris thought both purr and licks were the most wonderful things. He was a particular fan of all sub-vocal rumblings. The *isoga* of his own species made a similar noise when calming their young.

Elle had actually been hesitant when asking Tris to help with the cat. Not because she did not trust Tris, but because she thought Mister Montiguous might require too much effort.

"He can be such a bother, Tris love."

Tris had bounced on his heels, hair trembling in excitement. "It is a profound honor. You will show me everything to do with Mister Montiguous's maintenance and I shall be most diligent in his alimentation."

Elle had looked at him as if he were daft.

Tris was accustomed to that, from humans. His boss gave him that look nearly half a dozen times a day. But Tris was genuinely thrilled. After all, wasn't this the reason to live among aliens? To experience their foibles. Like tiny predators as pets. And honeymoons. Perhaps when Elle and Olav took their third honeymoon, they would let him join them and observe.

The first time Tris met Mister Montiguous, Tris had been, as Olav put it, *gobsmacked*. (A good word, that. Tris would have to find a moment to apply it himself. )

"But why do you *have* a \*cat\*neuter\*pet\*?" Tris kept asking them, after he determined the creature was not a new species of sentient alien. He would not want to offend the cat by talking about it, as if it could not participate in the conversation.

Mister Montiguous had a certain level of sentience, but not so that Tristol's diplomatic training need be applied.

"Because cats are great," Elle explained. "And they're one of the few pets not restricted to the home world." Apparently cats came from Hu-Core and had spread across the universe along with their human protectors.

They had been sitting in the humans' living room and *drinking tea* at the time, a ritual Tris found odd if enjoyable. Hot beverages as an instrument of welcome, fancy that? They were all watching the cat. Mister Montiguous performed some kind of interpretive dance move in pursuit of a tossed fluffy ball. Olav laughed and called him a *wonderful feline creature*.

"You keep it around for entertainment?" Tris had learned early on that there was very little humans would not do in pursuit of entertainment. (This also possibly explained all the progeny. ) They were easily entertained, especially, as it turned out, by Tris. It was a mutually beneficial arrangement. Tris was wildly curious and naturally flirty, and humans were easily flattered by both. Perhaps cats were the same.

Olav was good about explaining things once he knew Tristol was eager to learn. "Originally, cats went on ships for pest control. They're rather ferocious hunters, although you'd never know it looking at old Monty here. His most strenuous activity is eviscerating a bowl of protein sim."

Mister Montiguous stopped chasing the fluffy ball and flopped over in apparent exhaustion.

"It is marvelous," defended Tris, utterly charmed.

When Mister Montiguous staggered over to him, and pressed a furry face into the hand Tris offered, Tris fell in love. Physical affection was something he greatly missed. Humans were not nearly as *open*contact*touch* as the galoi. He missed that a lot, and this funny hairy beastie seemed to notice.

"You can pet him, Tris. Just down his back and then scratch about the ears. Exactly." Elle's eyes were pleased as Tristol worshiped her cat.

"It is so soft!"

"*He* is a *he*, Tris," Elle corrected, gently.

"But I thought you said it was a neuter?"

Olav laughed. "*Neutered,* not *neuter*. He has masculine parts. Well, some of them, just no longer the ability to procreate."

Tristol nodded. That made sense. The cat was like a *male isoga*, then. Physically male, only without the ability to inseminate like an *antiga*. Tris adjusted his vocabulary to the proper pronoun and worked hard to become very good friends with Mister Montiguous. *Male isoga* were often the most powerful of the galoi. He would not want to make a mistake with the cat equivalent.

Tris had been invited over to Elle and Olav's quarters for a meal (hot beverages came before food). It was his first time inside the private quarters of a human couple on a friendship basis. It was always amazing to see the inside workings of a human home. Tris would do anything not to offend and be dismissed. So he did exactly as Elle instructed and stroked the cat along the grain of his fur.

Mister Montiguous began to purr.

Tris decided that Mister Montiguous was the best thing in the whole galaxy.

Except for Detective Hastion, of course.

Detective Hastion made his hair *fluff*.

Now, several rotations later, Elle and Olav had invited Tris to cat-sit, and Tristol was beyond honored. Although *cat-sit* was another odd word. Tris hoped he was not meant to actually *sit* on top of Mister Montiguous. He did not think either of them would enjoy that. In fact, it seemed to work the other way around. The cat would occasionally sit atop him in some kind of primitive dominance display, as if Tristol were mere furniture designed specifically for one dictatorial carnivore. Tris accepted this status gravely.

He took his cat-sitting duty very seriously, more seriously than his actual professional job on the space station.

"You need to do *what*?" His \*human\*female\*boss\* Adjudicator Jones seemed more than unusually gobsmacked by his insistence. (*Such* a good word. )

"I must leave early, my boss," Tris said, clasping his fingers, bouncing only a little, and trying to control the rapidity of his breathing. He was about to go *feed a cat*! "I must go forthwith to bestow upon Mister Montiguous his protein supper. It is the hour of his consumption." Tristol tried to use big impressive words so his boss might understand how important this was.

"Who," Adjudicator Jones asked with slow confused gravity, "is Mister Montiguous?"

Tristol was amazed. "You have not met him? Oh but he is wonderful! He is…" he allowed a significant pause to draw out the verbal tension, "…a *feline*."

His boss did not seem suitably impressed. "You need to leave early to feed a cat?"

"Yes! Do you not see how important it is? I have been given sacred charge of a beloved human pet. He is a delicate thing. I must take the greatest of care with him."

"Tristol, it's just a cat."

Tris did not understand such a dismissive attitude.

"Oh, stop looking at me with such big wounded eyes. Go on, then." She flapped her hand at him. "Wait."

Tris paused before sprinting out the door.

"Don't forget your com pad."

Tristol's hair wilted slightly in embarrassment. "Oh dear. Of course not." He gathered up his small portable computing device and other necessary communication equipment from his desk, as he was supposed to do every night.

The adjudicator merely looked affectionately amused. "How long will you have care of this cat?" *How long,* he knew she was really asking, *will you be so scattered?*

"Six whole days!" Tris tried to impress upon her the significance of the responsibility. "I am the only one they asked. Such a privilege."

His boss looked as if she were trying not to laugh. She did that a lot around him. Tris thought, sometimes, it was one of the reasons she hired him. Humans and their love of entertainment.

He was also an excellent diplomatic negotiator and cultural mediator, of course. He was, after all, *loga*. Those few galoi who left Gal were in high demand because they were all *loga*, and *loga* got along well with every other species. *Loga* got along with *everyone*. Except for the *pakaa nova*. But then no one got along with them. And even pakaa nova were still more likely to talk to a galoi than any other alien.

Most species also thought galoi were cute and unthreatening. Big round eyes, excitable hair, and purple tones apparently conveyed wonder and innocence. Tristol would take what he could get.

Humans also thought the galoi were sexy.

Tris thought this was *great*.

But right now he had a cat to feed.

Mister Montiguous was waiting impatiently for Tris when he keyed into Olav and Elle's quarters.

This was yet another way in which humans were odd. Galoi were a communal species. They tended to eat together in large groups. Grooming and bathing were also cooperative activities. Basically, *everything* was done in the common nests. In fact, a private residence was mainly for sleeping and the associated pleasure activities of a spousal group.

Humans, being weird, had their living quarters divided into named zones: the bathroom, the living room, the kitchen, and so forth. Tris found this challenging. His own residence felt big and empty and solitary. Although his human friends assured him that space station quarters were considered very cramped by planet-side standards.

The living room area of Olav and Elle's home belonged to Mister Montiguous. It was this zone that the door opened onto. It consisted of a semi-private section where the spousal group ate, occasionally welcoming *select* friends to eat alongside. There was a seating area, or living room, for when they *entertained*, as Elle called it (there is that word again).

One of Tristol's other human friendship groups was made up of three males who lived together. On Tristol's planet these would have been instantly designated a spousal group, but they were actually something called *platonic roommates* and did not share sexual relations. They had invited Tristol over to a *game night*. Tristol had learned the word *game* could imply bed cuddles and sex, but not in this context, as it turned out. Game night had also not involved a meal but instead *snacks* combined with a shared endeavor involving cards with pictures and an imaginary verbally hallucinated reality. That also had taken place in the living room. So Tris supposed living rooms must be human halfway spaces, neither public nor private but somehow both.

He wondered what Detective Hastion did in his living room.

One of the things Elle and Olav did in theirs, besides invite Tris over to feed him regularly, because they said he seemed a little lonely (which he probably was) and ill-equipped to cook for himself (which he definitely was), was keep their cat.

Mister Montiguous, home alone without his humans, was gratifyingly pleased to see Tristol. The moment Tris was inside, the cat lumbered over to twine about his legs.

Tris assumed this was an attempt to trip him so he might fall and be on the cat's same level.

Tris dropped his communication devices and, to save himself from injury, crouched down to cede to the cat's demands.

He scratched Mister Montiguous around the ears, as required. Tris understood that – he too liked to be petted about the ears.

Mister Montiguous purred.

Tris was happy.

Which is why he must be excused for not immediately turning to seal the door behind him.

When the very loud blare of a perimeter alarm emanated throughout the station, it startled Mister Montiguous. The cat darted, not back into the safety of his home, but out into the hallway of the greater space station.

Tris, in a total panic, chased after him.

Olav had told Tris that Mister Montiguous was considered rather fat for a cat. But Mister Montiguous could still move quickly when he put his mind to it.

The carnivore took off down the hallway in an expeditious waddle. Unfortunately, he chose the direction of the central area where all the dining carts were located, and not away into the warren of residences.

The station was set up like a huge spinning sphere, generating artificial gravity but also providing the kind of circular comfort all species enjoyed. Every race in the galaxy, after all, originated on a *round* planet. Spheres, therefore, were considered the most cross-cultural psychologically satisfying shape.

The humans built their space stations so that every zone was a mix of public and private, with the more public toward the core. The very center was equipped with a gravity-free float-hub where one could drift up, down, sideways, or anything in between, in order to get between zones.

Work areas and the things that actually ran the station, like docking bays, were all located on the station's crust. It was common for the residents of any one particular zone to also work and socialize in that same zone. The humans did this by design.

Apparently, it had been determined that human socialization numbers over one hundred and fifty were untenable, so residence warrens were kept to one fifty and no more. Tris rather liked this. He found it comforting to see familiar faces as he walked to work each day, even if they were alien faces.

Of course, people always drifted between zones. The best pub – for example, the one that catered to non-humans (through the simple expedient of stocking a range of alien beverages) – was located in Zone 6. Elle and Olav lived in Zone 3, like Tris. In fact, he had met them in what humans called the *local park*, a kind of communal social eating area with cultivated vegetation close to the grav-free hub.

So when Mister Montiguous took off toward that very hub, Tris was familiar with the terrain. He was also familiar with most of the people around him as he ran.

Tris moved fast. He wanted to catch Mister Montiguous before the cat reached the transport hub. He had no idea how a cat would react to lack of gravity, but he was certain he should not unleash something with such sharp claws and no sense of personal-body etiquette into a busy float-hub.

So he was desperate to catch the cat. Unfortunately, the cat was desperate to get away from the noise. Which was still blaring all around them and could not be escaped. *Silly cat.*

"Hey Tris, where you off to?" asked *human*female*neighbor* Mrs Ullriche.

"I am trying to catch that cat, Mrs Ullriche," replied Tris politely. "Sorry, I can not stop." He sprinted on. "Tomorrow, may I bring by that berry I found at the market for identification?"

The elderly human was a botanist and fruit aficionado. She grinned at him and waved. "Of course, sweet boy!"

Tris waved back and ran on, hoping he had not been too rude.

"Is that Tris? Watch out, Tris! You shouldn't run in the—"

"Hello Mr Churig! I am sorry, but I have a cat to catch.

Did you see…? Oh, there he is! Stop! Mister Montiguous! Bad kitty!"

Mister Montiguous was clearly not one for following instructions. He took a flying leap upward, higher than Tris thought he could jump, and was now toddle-dashing across the awning of a food stall in the hawker center.

Tris loved the stalls. He ate there every day (when his human friends did not invite him into their living rooms). Galoi had no known food allergies and notoriously resilient stomachs (two of them). He had tried every possible cuisine on the space station, from the wide range offered by humans with their innumerable cultures, to food from other alien species. In consequence, Tristol knew most of the hawkers and they knew him.

People cried his name in welcome. It often took him hours to get a meal because he made a point of stopping and chatting with all the cooks. (Unless the line was long and they were busy, of course. )

But today his behavior would appear off. He was trotting along eyes up, watching as the cat leapt from one awning to the next. The coverings were merely for show, colored cloth stretched across frames. Tris was certain that at any moment Mister Montiguous would fall right through one of them. He would be hurt! It would be *awful*. Tris was prepared to leap forward and catch him. But so far the cat kept up a brisk enough pace not to rip through.

Eventually the food stalls ended and Mister Montiguous stopped in the far corner of the awning of the very last stall. It was a ramen vendor. Ramen was a kind of soup which Tristol thought delicious and ate regularly. He was charmed by noodles in general, partly because they reminded him of galoi hair. Consequently, he knew the *human-dorien*female?*cook* Mistress Zing well. Xe was split-species, probably about his own age, although difficult to tell. Tris had gotten relatively good at estimating human ages, but he was not as adept with other aliens. He thought Mistress Zing quite pretty with xer long gray hair and silver skin covered in a dorien's indented texture. Xer flesh had less contrast than in a full-blooded dorien, which always looked to Tris as if someone had stamped feathers into skin. Felt that way too. Delightful. He was fond of dorien when he could find one to play with.

Mistress Zing had once expressed admiration for Tristol and invited him to a sexual liaison.

Tris had explained that he was not attracted to biologically presenting females. He had touched his naked ear, where he once wore a single black ring. The earring had identified him as sexually attracted only to *antiga*. The closest term the humans had, with their limited understanding of gender, was *homosexual*.

Fortunately, Mistress Zing had not taken offense and only laughed. "All the good ones are gay, huh? Should've known. You're too pretty for words."

Tristol did not explain the difference between *male loga* and gay. He was *zyga* now anyway, anathema to his people, genderless by virtue of exile. He was, socially speaking, no longer *loga* at all. Yet here he stood, light years away and a decade off Gal, and his ear still felt barren without its ring.

He consoled himself that he never lacked for male company. Even if none of them wished to keep him. He had managed to understand and successfully execute several sexual encounters, much to his enjoyment and that of his partners, but beyond that none wished to stay with him for any length of time. He had never been offered a spousal contract. Perhaps he was doing it wrong.

He gave Mistress Zing a brief appraising look. Perhaps he could overlook her lack of male genitalia? Then he laughed at himself. Like any *loga* could change his rings. His ears may be naked, but he still wore the black coil of metal on a cord around his neck. Tucked under his clothing.

Tonight Mistress Zing had a line for ramen. But Tristol thought an escaped cat was important enough to break one of the human's most sacred taboos, so he jumped the queue. He felt compelled to alert Mistress Zing to the fact that there was a cat above xer that may fall into xer broth pot at any moment.

"I am all apologies, Mistress Zing, but Mister Montiguous is on your awning and I am responsible for his recapture."

Mistress Zing looked up, startled. "Mister Monti- guous?"

Tris explained the only way he knew how. "*Cat*neuter*pet*."

The vendor looked started. "There is a cat on my roof?"

Tristol nodded vigorously. "I do beg your pardon. He is in my care. I am afraid the alarm startled him."

He noticed, at that moment, that the alarm had stopped blaring. He wondered what was so important the whole station had been put on alert. Then he worried he might be needed. His contact devices – which his boss always insisted, *Tristol, please, keep at least one on you at all times!* – were all back in Elle and Olav's living room. Perhaps the alarm indicated the need for an adjudicator attaché. He might be in even more trouble than he was already.

Then, suddenly, he *was* in even *more* trouble.

Because Tristol's favorite *human*male*sexy-stroke-him-all-over* showed up and growled at him.

"What are you up to now, Mr Zyga?" Detective Hastion was always growling at Tris.

Tristol glanced away from the cat – he could not help it, Detective Hastion was *so* pretty. He wore his customary dark gray security uniform and his equally customary human frown. Detective Hastion always frowned at Tris. It went with the growling.

All those aspects of Tristol's character, and species, and gender that everyone else seemed to find so appealing, Detective Hastion found annoying. Tristol, of course, could not help himself, and became even more, well, *more everything*, around the detective. Because Detective Hastion was the hottest thing Tristol had ever seen in his whole life and that included the *antiga* of his own species.

Tris admired everything about the detective, from the rumbly voice to the very short dark hair and slightly darker eyes. The human's skin was dark too, and not in the deep purple way of *antiga*, but more a warm brown. It looked impossibly warm and soft and Tristol wanted to rub up against him. It was embarrassing (or it would be if any galoi ever saw him in the human's company) because Tristol could not hide his reaction. His hair got all puffy and reached out to twine about the detective whenever he was near.

Just finding him standing there behind him made Tristol's breathing go shallow. Tris had to smother the need to sidle up to the big human and *touch*stroke* twine*lick*.

Detective Hastion also had hair growing on his face, which was a thing some human males did called bearding. Tris thought beards might be ritualized or seasonal, like birds molting. The galoi did not have hair anywhere but on their heads, and that was not exactly *hair* by human standards.

Galoi hair was a living thing, thick and tubular (like noodles) and quite sensitive to touch. Tristol's own hair was considered very attractive by his species, or so he had been told before he left Gal. It was long and lush and a rich lavender color, only a shade darker than his skin and a shade lighter than his eyes. He was so vain about his hair, he had chosen his advocate partly because her hair color almost perfectly matched his. That strand of advocacy was gone now, sadly, but Tris was still vain about his hair.

Detective Hastion, much to Tristol's sadness, was totally immune to every last purple piece of Tristol's noodley lavender hair.

# THE 2<sup>ND</sup> CHAPTER

## *In danger of cat scratches and ramen splashes*

There was some kind of commotion in the hawker center.

This was annoying, as Drey was hungry and technically off duty. All he wanted was ramen and bed.

The commotion was at the ramen stall and at the center of it was, no surprise to Drey, Tristol Zyga.

Since he'd moved aboard the station, Mr Zyga had been a thorn in Drey's side. Of course, everyone *adored* Mr Zyga.

Drey also adored him – that was part of the problem.

My Zyga (and Drey would think of him that way or die trying) was galoi, so of course everyone adored him. Considering how few galoi moved off planet, the station was incredibly lucky to have one in residence.

There was something about galoi. They comforted by their very presence. They were friendly and amusing and fun and generous. They were charming and smart – eager to learn about others. All qualities any space station would want on their payroll. Also, a galoi off Gal was a certified exile with no possibility of ever returning, thus entirely lacking in planetary allegiance. This made them the perfect neutral party, a major political asset.

Everyone liked a galoi.

Everyone on Station XO17 loved Mr Zyga.

Drey avoided him like a dorien mega plague.

Yet Mr Zyga always seemed to be in trouble. Or in the middle of some dramatic emotional crisis over flower petals. Or causing a ruckus with noodles. Or starting a dance party. Or creating the universe's first flower petal noodle dance extravaganza. Also, he was the most fucking adorable thing Drey had ever seen in his life.

Mr Zyga was about as high as Drey's shoulder, his body smooth and sleek. He was also purple. Actually goddam purple!

After meeting Tris – no, *Mr Zyga* – Drey had gone home to his quarters and stroked off (because *look* at him), cleaned himself up in disgust, and then searched for as much information as he could find on the galoi.

There was very little known about them.

The planet of Gal was xenophobic in the extreme. What little was known about the galoi had been gathered via very limited remote trade relations, and the hundred or so exiles who fled their planet for a life in the stars. Those exiles were remarkably close-mouthed.

What Drey managed to find out was that the galoi had five genders. *Five!* Pictures of other exiles showed all galoi had the same heart-shaped faces with big rounder-than-human eyes, sweet smiles with pointed teeth, and large pointed ears. Basically: grape-flavored super hot elves with sea-anemone hair.

Drey was a devout scuba diver, had a horrible sweet tooth, and his favorite flavor was grape.

Of course, since Drey was wildly attracted to Mr Zyga, dealing with him on a professional basis was that much more challenging. So Drey defaulted to stiff and grumpy.

Mr Zyga only ever gave Drey the same open, friendly treatment he gave everyone.

Which annoyed Drey further, because more than anything else he would like to be special to this man, to be treated differently. But Tris was galoi, notoriously promiscuous (that was in all the files, because it might cause an international incident). Drey, on the other hand, knew himself well enough to identify as quite gay, quite monogamous, and probably too domineering and possessive for most modern human men, let alone a galoi.

Which is why he was left merely imagining what lavender skin tasted like, and forcing his attraction to convert to annoyance whenever he ran into Mr Zyga.

Of course, they lived in the same zone.

Of course, it would be Mr Zyga causing a commotion at the ramen stand.

Of course, Drey would be the only security officer around to deal with it.

He couldn't help it – he growled. "What are you up to now, Mr Zyga?"

Tristol gave a little shiver and turned around.

Drey hoped he hadn't frightened him.

The galoi blinked at him a moment out of those impossibly big purple eyes. Then he gave Drey one of his charming pointed smiles. His amazing hair, much thicker than a human's – like the stem of a plant – drifted toward Drey, as if pushed by a wind that wasn't there.

"Detective! How lovely. Could you call me Tristol or even Tris, please? I have asked you before. I do not like Mr Zyga." He looked briefly a little sad.

"It's your name, isn't it?"

"Not *exactly*. It is more a title. We do not really have last names."

Drey remembered reading that all galoi in exile took the last name Zyga in order to integrate better with humans and human classification systems. There were arguments among academics as to why the word Zyga and what exactly it meant.

Drey crossed his arms and stepped back, out of reach of Tristol's hair which had, apparently of its own volition, started to caress Drey's forearm. It was very soft and his skin tingled at the touch.

Mr Zyga seemed to be trying to glare at his own hair. "Sorry about that, detective. It can be difficult around you."

Drey snorted. Too bad it was only Mr Zyga's hair that Drey managed to distract – he'd love to distract the rest of him.

Tris thought Detective Hastion was something distractingly special.

He was big. On the largest end of the spectrum for a human, which meant huge for a galoi. He had lots of muscles, too, plus the hair on his face, all of which made him very exotic. Also galoi considered it aesthetically pleasing to be generally in the same color palette. It had taken Tris a long time to get accustomed to those humans who had sharply contrasting skin and hair and eyes. It was so jarring. But the detective was all lovely shades of warm dark brown, deep and comforting and almost familiar, in the way of an *antiga*. Only better. Because there was more of him and not all-over purple. Purple reminded Tris too much of home and things he had lost, or more properly, given up.

Of course, Tristol's stupid hair betrayed him the moment the detective was near. He just found the human too attractive to control his hair. Which, frankly, had never happened to him before – like he was a juvenile in his first estrus.

And now the human was giving him that growly official look that said he was annoyed, not to mention a member of the station's security force, so Tris better fess up to his latest mistake.

Instead Tris wondered if Drey had progeny. Had he given his three to the betterment of his species? Had he done his duty? Was that even a requirement for humans?

He bet Detective Hastion had gifted his people with beautiful younglings.

Tris was caught up just looking at the human. Which meant he was growled at again and had forgotten about the cat.

Tris loved the growling. It was a little like an *isoga's* comfort rumble. And at least the detective felt enough for him to growl. Annoyance was not the emotion he desired most from the big human, but he would take it if that was all he could get.

Tris tried to explain. "It is Mister Montiguous, you see? He got away. And I chased him here. And now he is in danger of falling into the soup." Tris thought this was all pretty self-explanatory, seeing as the cat was still sitting in his precarious position on top of the noodle stand.

Except that the detective gave him the look that said Tris was unhinged. "What? Who? Montiguous?"

"Mister Montiguous is a cat," explained Mistress Zing, continuing to serve ramen as though xe were not in grave danger of being splashed and scalded.

Mister Montiguous was looking less scared and more miffed to find himself in a ramen-scented predicament. He glared down at Tris from his superior position, yellow eyes accusatory. *How could Tris have allowed this to happen? And why did Tris not get him down?*

Detective Hastion did not take his eyes off Tris.

Tristol pointed up to the cat.

The detective's gaze followed his finger and then he snorted. "Mr Zyga, pets aren't allowed out of private quarters."

"I know, detective. That is why I was chasing him."

"Well, catch him then and take him home."

"I can not reach." Tris applied his big eyes to the human in a pleading manner. He had been told by more than one human lover that his eyes were his best feature. Although one had really liked his hair, especially wrapped around his penis. Tris wondered if Detective Hastion would like such a thing. Several strands fluttered in the human's direction again. Tris tried to clamp down on both thoughts and hair.

The eyes clearly did something because Drey swallowed, looked away, and seemed to get even more annoyed.

*Oh dear,* thought Tris.

"Fine," Detective Hastion grumbled. "I'll handle it."

He was tall enough too.

He simply marched over, reached up, and grabbed the affronted Mister Montiguous by the scruff of his furry neck.

Mister Montiguous was having none of it. He had never met Detective Hastion. They had not been introduced. Yet here he was being summarily manhandled by the human.

Tris could not understand it at all. He would give anything to be manhandled by Detective Hastion.

Mister Montiguous, however, clearly did not feel the same. Because he yowled, struggled, and scratched poor Detective Hastion on his forearms.

Tris whimpered in horror and sympathy.

But Detective Hastion clearly was a soldier at heart, because he held on and did not even wince.

Tris was impressed.

Drey could take or leave cats, to be honest. He'd met some nice ones, he'd met some asshole ones. Same with dogs. This one was clearly an asshole. But Drey wasn't stupid enough to let the creature go once he had hold of him. Better to take the scratches and deal with returning the beastie back home. This was an attitude that had served Drey well throughout his career, earning him the reputation for being a hard-ass – relentless in his cases as a detective and steady in his rounds when he'd been a beat cop planet-side. As station security, his world was now a bit of both patrol and detective work. He liked the variety and he could withstand a few scratches.

Besides, Mr Zyga was looking at him like he was the

strongest, most heroic man ever to walk a space station.

"Are you not hurting?" The galoi's big eyes were even bigger than normal in apparent awe.

"Yes it fucking hurts. Now show me where he belongs so I can put him down."

Pretty Mr Zyga jumped and bobbed his head. "Oh goodness, yes! You should follow me, please. Goodbye Mistress Zing. This way, detective, to the living quarters of my friends. And privacy. Just me and you... and Mister Montiguous." The man was muttering to himself now and moving toward one of the residential sections. "Is this romantic?" He looked back at Drey and moved faster. "Does the presence of Mister Montiguous make us being together more or less romantic by human standards?"

Drey shook his head. Tristol Zyga was a wack job, but the cutest purplest wack job ever. So Drey trailed after him, clutching the hissing spitting clawing creature and trying not to notice how unbelievably graceful the galoi was, and how he had the perkiest little ass Drey had ever seen.

The walk was a revelation. Every few steps someone called a greeting and Mr Zyga would pause to chat.

"How are you, Mr Churig? Is Mrs Churig feeling any better today?"

Brief exchange of pleasantries.

Walk on.

"Not my cat, thank you for asking. The detective is being very nice and responsible and helping me get him back to safety."

And again.

"Not at the moment, Mrs Ullriche, thank you. Why yes! We *are* going back to the cat's place of residence *together*. Yes, he *is* very handsome! I could not agree more. You do not know Detective Hastion? Oh, you mean the cat is handsome."

And so on.

They made it back to residential quarters. Eventually.

Mr Zyga had left the door open. Drey shook his head, grateful *that* particular kind of security wasn't much of an issue on this station. Still, perhaps he should remind the galoi about safety precautions.

"This your place?" he couldn't help but ask.

The galoi's hair flattened.

Drey had no idea what that meant but he suspected embarrassment.

"Oh no, detective! It is nice though, is it not?" Genuine curiosity was in his voice.

Drey shrugged. He wasn't much interested in interior design. One set of standard quarters looked pretty much like another to him. "It's fine."

Tris nodded earnestly. "It belongs to *humans*female-male*heterosexual-spouses*friends* Elle and Olav."

Tristol did that sometimes, mashed together the identification of person plus species and gender. It was endearing and clearly some remnant from his native language. Drey wondered how Tris might talk about or introduce Drey to others: *acquaintance*male* single*grumpy* perhaps?

"Seal the door, please, Mr Zyga."

The pretty man jumped to do so and Drey was finally able to drop the cat. The cat had the affront to then bunt up against Drey's legs as if he hadn't just gouged multiple long scratches into his arms.

Drey glared down at him.

Mr Zyga's voice was hesitant. "I do not know the proper etiquette. Do I invite you to sit down in quarters that are not my own? Would that be rude to you or to *Elle*Olav*?"

Drey finally put everything together.

It's not that he was slow, just that he found Tris – argh, *Mr Zyga* – hugely confusing. Add that to his attraction, and Drey spent most of his time around the galoi in a state of heightened arousal and distraction.

"You're cat-sitting for some friends and the cat escaped?"

Mr Zyga bounced on his toes. "Yes! I did not know he could *do* that. The alarm startled him. Oh, the alarm! I should check—" And just like that the galoi was sidetracked by some other thought.

*Flighty*, thought Drey, wistfully. Was that a bad thing? It was probably just his species nature to be mercurial. Mr Zyga wasn't disloyal. The adjudicator spoke very highly of her attaché whenever she ran into Drey socially. He was good at his job, so everyone said. Not that Drey had asked about him, of course. The conversation just naturally wended its way to Mr Zyga. But he did come off as flighty.

Mister Montiguous, as if he hadn't caused a fuss, left off sniffing Drey's boots to swagger toward the kitchen with his tail up.

Mr Zyga was crouched down and rummaging frantically through what looked to be his work bag, discarded on the floor. So Drey followed the cat into the kitchen.

The cat yapped at him.

Drey took that to mean it was dinner time.

Suddenly Mr Zyga was close, long fingers floating over Drey's arms, skimming his skin, carefully avoiding the scratches, electric and tantalizing. It seemed to be a subconscious caress, merely letting Drey know he was present, because he stopped when the cat meowed imperiously.

He and Drey switched places in the small kitchen so Mr Zyga could attend to the creature.

Drey wondered if the silky texture of Mr Zyga's lavender skin was the same all over. He wanted to press up against him, slide his hands under that natty suit, and find out.

He moved away.

"Oh! I am *so* bad at this. Mister Montiguous, you

require your meal and I forgot." Tris put down his communicator, obviously the thing he'd been frantically searching for, so he could locate a pouch of protein sim and rip it open.

The com was blinking rapidly, indicating an urgent message.

Tris cared more about the stupid cat.

"Mr Zyga?"

"Tris, please, detective. Or Tristol if you must. Zyga is uncomfortable."

"Why?"

Tris dumped the sim into the cat's dish and spread it out carefully, before placing it in front of the impatient animal. He watched the cat eat for a moment and then he stared at the empty package in his hand.

"What was I to do with this? Did I ask Olav? I forgot to ask."

He turned pleading eyes on Drey, who shook his head, hid a smile, and showed him how to use the recycling unit.

"Oh!" Tris was delighted with this. "I have one of those!"

"You've been on this station for months and you've never used your recycling unit?"

Tristol's hair collapsed and he almost whispered, melodic voice crestfallen, "I do not use my kitchen at all. I do not know how."

Drey was aghast. He loved to cook. "What do you eat?"

"Everything! Only, you know, out there." Tris gestured back the way they'd come. "I even visit other zones to try *all* the different foods. It is wonderful." His hair floated up slightly and the tips of his ears twitched.

His glee was almost painful to witness. To take such joy in something as mundane as food. Drey could feel himself harden just from knowing the man was happy. "Why don't you like the name *Zyga*?"

Mr Zyga looked away, hair instantly wilted, not as still

as it was when he was ashamed, but more limp and sad.

Drey hated the very idea that anything could make this vibrant creature sad.

"Zyga is a non-title. A denial of existence. It implies exile, but more like your older term *outcaste*. A *zyga* has no identity, no role in society, no gender. We are anathema. Utterly rejected."

Drey knew some of that. He knew that a galoi off Gal could never return home. It was part of what made them safe as cultural attachés. He'd not realized it made them tantamount to non-persons in the eyes of their own species. "You've no legal standing, no identity – nothing?"

Mr Zyga nodded. "Exactly. A *zyga* is nothing."

Drey thought he might start referring to Tristol by his first name and hang the intimacy. He would just have to deal with it. If *Zyga* made this lovely man sad, then he wouldn't use the word. He strove to understand further. "What happens if you meet another galoi?"

"To meet another *zyga* like myself would be a comfort but also a sorrow. We would understand what we both have lost but would share choice and purpose. He or she would be another *loga*, the same as me and thus not sexually compatible. If you are asking if we might form a union, that would not be possible." Tris seemed eager to explain at least this part.

Drey frowned. "Is that why *loga* are exiled? You're not sexually attracted to your own species?" He'd seen Tristol at some of the clubs. He didn't want to, of course, but he had. Tris had always come directly up to Drey, the moment he noticed him, and tried to flirt. Tried *hard*. Drey liked that, too much, but he'd never taken Tristol home. Just rebuffed him as gently as possible, and then spent a miserable evening watching Tristol, hair limp, wander around until he found some other man to leave with. Usually human.

Tris was looking at him, hair puffy but still.

Drey didn't know what that meant.

Fortunately Tris explained. "No! I mean, I like human males very much. But I find my own species attractive too. My preference is for *antiga*, a narrow choice, but common in *male loga*. I wear the black earring. Or, I should say that I once wore it. But that is not the reason for my exile. My people would lose many of their *loga* if it were. And we already struggle with population growth. No, I was expelled, like all *zyga,* because I refused *gamein."*

Drey was utterly confused. He'd no idea what the difference was between *loga* and *antiga*. He knew there were five genders on Gal and these must be two of them. Humans had only ever learned the names of three: *loga, antiga,* and *isoga.* But there didn't seem to be a visual cue as to what each meant, none seemed to correspond to female or male, and the other two remained unnamed. Galoi, when in contact with humans, always spoke in terms of *he* or *she*, as if they were binary. It drove anthropologists bonkers.

But the *zyga* that humans encountered refused to explain. Drey suspected he'd gotten more out of Tris in the last few minutes than any anthropologist ever. He wondered if he should report the information to someone, but that felt a little like a betrayal of Tristol's confidence.

He tried to keep the lines of communication open, though. Tris was being responsive and Drey was wildly curious. He wanted to know everything about this man, even if Tris was incapable of loving Drey as he wanted. Drey couldn't simply turn off his fascination.

"What does *gamein* mean? I never saw it in my research."

Tristol perked up, stopped watching the cat eat, and turned his big eyes back to Drey. "You researched galoi?"

Drey nodded, embarrassed.

Tristol stepped a little closer. "Because of me?" His hair fluffed up high and his eyes were bright.

Drey loved that he'd somehow expunged the sadness. "Your people are mysterious and fascinating."

Tris grinned. "Am *I* mysterious and fascinating?"

Drey copped out of that one. "I'm a detective. We're naturally pretty curious."

Tris nodded and shifted a little closer, placing a tentative hand on Drey's forearm, avoiding the scratches. "Yes?"

Drey had his arms crossed, because he really wanted to reach for Tristol.

The touch of the alien was needed and lovely. His skin was cool – well, cooler than a human's.

Drey nodded to the counter where Tristol's communicator blinked aggressively. "Don't you need to check your com?"

Tris swore in his own language, or Drey assumed that's what it was. A musical, lilting tongue.

Tristol picked up his con-com and listened. He wore no ear insert. Drey thought this might be because they didn't make them to fit the shape of a galoi's pointed ear. Or perhaps Tristol's ears were too sensitive.

Drey moved away to give the man privacy and tapped his own ear-com. "Detective Hastion reporting in. I'm off duty at the moment but that alarm was a sixer, so I'm obligated to check."

The voice of dispatch snorted at him. "Little late, aren't you?"

Drey only snorted back.

"Stand by, detective." A pause. "You're on reserve. The nature of the emergency is not yet determined. Don't leave the station for any reason."

Drey grunted. "I never leave the station."

Drey loved his job. He rarely took vacation or went planet-side. Alevon Two, the nearest habitable planet, was a stupid world anyway. Mostly small tropical islands with luxury hotels and no interesting underwater sea life. Drey just wasn't a fruity-drinks-on-the-beach kinda dude. The tiny paper umbrellas bothered him. Besides, why should he leave the station? Tris was here.

Speaking of, the lavender-colored beauty had finished his call and was looking even more frantic than usual.

"Oh, dear. Mister Montiguous has not yet been played with or petted and I have been summoned to my job with great urgency. The adjudicator *yelled* at my com unit! She seemed most frustrated that I did not pick up the moment she pinged. I should go. But the cat has not been tended and I promised so faithfully."

Drey rolled his eyes. "I'll stay with the cat."

"And you will play with him and pet him and tell him he's a *wonderful feline creature*?"

"He's *not* a wonderful feline creature. Did you forget the mad ramen escape? But yes, I'll play with him. Show me his toys."

Tristol smiled.

Until Tris, smiling was something Drey had thought of as a human trait. For most aliens the showing of teeth was an aggressive move, indicating anger. Or hunger. But Tristol Zyga, galoi, smiled all the damn time.

"Detective, I knew you could not be *all* grumpy. Do you need tending?"

Drey's cock jumped at the offer until he realized Tristol's big eyes were on Drey's crossed arms. *The cat scratches.* He'd stopped bleeding but the evidence of Mister Montiguous's ill favor was still obvious.

Drey tried not to bask in the alien's concern. What might it be like to come back this man at the end of each shift and know he was cared for? Glorious.

"It is literally nothing more than a scratch. I've had worse from cactus."

"What is a cat-tus?"

"A kind of sharp, spiny plant. Hardy but vicious."

"Is it named after cats?"

Drey chuckled. "No, but it should be."

"You will be well then? From Mister Montiguous's abuse?"

"I'll be fine."

Tristol smiled again and handed Drey a long stick with a piece of string and a bit of feather at the end.

"I'm fishing for cats?"

"I do not know what that means, but you wave the stick and he will jump after it. It is most amusing."

Tristol gathered up his bag and a few other scattered items near the door. Clearly they'd been dropped in lieu of cat pursuit.

He turned back to Drey. "You will stay here and cat-sit for me?"

"I will."

"Until I get back? You will wait for me?"

"I will."

Tristol looked thrilled. "That is *wonderful*." He made a funny hand gesture. "May I?"

Drey didn't know what it meant, so he shrugged.

Tris darted at him and then pressed the side of his face to Drey's. He rubbed against Drey's beard as if reveling in the texture.

Drey supposed it must be a galoi gesture of farewell.

Tris gave a little trill noise of pleasure.

Drey wondered if he made that noise at other times. Then stopped himself from that line of thought or he might embarrass both of them.

"You are so beautiful." Tristol whispered.

A ridiculous statement, as Tris was obviously the beautiful one.

The galoi drew back, looking happy. "You will be here when I return?" He asked again.

Drey nodded.

"Thank you." Tristol's words were heartfelt.

Drey wondered if he'd agreed to something *more*. It

was too late to ask. Or to explain that if he was called to duty he absolutely wouldn't be able to wait and play with the dumb cat, because Tristol had darted out into the hallway and disappeared.

He left the door open behind him again.

It was a good thing Drey was station security – quite apart from everything else, he could override the seal.

He sighed and went to close the door, while the dumb cat was still chowing down on his food.

Mister Montiguous, indeed! What a name for a cat.

# THE 3<sup>RD</sup> CHAPTER

## *It's always better to have puffy hair*

Adjudicator Jones was pacing the office in evident annoyance when Tristol finally hurried inside.

"Where have you been?"

"Mister Montiguous escaped and went to visit ramen and Detective Hastion had to catch him."

"Tris, you can just say *the cat*. You don't have to call him by name."

"But that would be rude!" objected Tris. "It is such a very good name: Mister Montiguous."

His boss gave him a sly look. "Not Drey Hastion?"

"That is a good name too. Is *Drey* Detective Hastion's preliminary moniker?" Tristol tried it out on his tongue to see if it worked. It did. It suited Detective Hastion and he liked it very much. "Do you think he would let me call him Drey sometime?"

"I think the good detective would let you call him anything you wanted."

Tris suspected Adjudicator Jones of teasing him, since he had no idea what this meant. He offered, proudly. "I left him looking after Mister Montiguous. He even said he would wait for me to return."

The adjudicator seemed to approve. "Progress at last."

Again Tris did not know what she meant by that, but it sounded good. "I like him very much," he confessed.

"I know you do, sweetie. However your love life will have to remain unresolved for the moment, as you were supposed to be here a half hour ago because we have need of your skills."

Tris was instantly all business. "Diplomacy or negotiation?"

"Bit of both. But it's actually your origins that are needed."

"My origins, adjudicator?"

Adjudicator Jones had tried to get him to call her by her first name at the office, but Tris felt that it would not be right. He knew human etiquette in this matter, since he had worked in some capacity or another for a human boss ever since he left his own planet. It was not correct to be overly familiar in the work space. He was always good about calling her Areletta when in an informal social environment, though. It was not a name he thought suited her, but she obviously wished him to use it, so he did. But only when appropriate.

Areletta Jones was a tall, imposing individual. Her skin was a light brown, and her hair was a sharp contrasting yellow, which Tris believed was by artifice rather than nature. At first it made him wince because it clashed with her skin tone, but he'd learned other humans thought this combination aesthetically pleasing. She had sharp features and a wide mouth with lots of square teeth which made her look rather fierce. Except her laugh was loud and joyful and frequent.

Tristol admired her greatly but he did not think her pretty, not by his species' standards. She did very well for herself, though. Tris had met both her husbands and both were charming and devoted and quite loving to her and each other, in the manner that one always dreams spouses ought to be. Tristol himself had only ever wanted one spouse, a perversion in the eyes of his own culture, but that did not stop him from being happy for others' capacity to collect.

He had been invited to dine with the Joneses on several occasions and always enjoyed it immensely. They'd never invited him into the bed chamber with them for genital play, for which he was faintly relieved and also a little insulted. Perhaps three was a *cota* for humans? Elle and Olav had invited him into their bed. He'd declined, of course. Olav was hot, but Tris was not attracted to females, and it was bad form to participate in a sexual encounter with *two* when he was only interested in *one*. Everyone knew that. He thought this was likely a universal truth.

All this to say that Tris thought of his boss as \*human\*female\*friend\* as well as superior, but in the confines of the office he preferred to think of her as \*human\*female\*boss\*. So he used her title as a form of address, and she reluctantly accepted that as a quirk of his character.

He thought of Adjudicator Jones as rather like a human version of a *female isoga*. The adjudicator was tough and almost military in her outlook, but caring – a protector.

"Please explain, adjudicator?"

"The alarm, did you hear it?"

"Everyone heard it, including Mister Montiguous, who took grave offense."

"It was a hostile proximity alert. An alien spaceship approached the station without authorization. Initially, we had issues with contact and communication. We eventually managed it through the aid of a digital drone. The ship has proved unthreatening, we think, but it has made a rather unusual request."

Tristol was all business. "What species of ship?"

He was already mentally preparing himself to open negotiations. What level of empathy might be required of him? How would he phrase the greeting, depending on the species? He began to catalogue those aliens with whom he knew humans had contentious relationships.

His boss stopped his thoughts with the one phrase

guaranteed to shock.

"They're galoi."

Tristol could feel his hair flattening, fast and stiff. Not in shame this time, but fear. Not that the galoi would necessarily do anything to *him*. He no longer existed for them. He would be ignored. It was just that the idea of seeing his people again without the benefit of status was daunting. Especially since he had lost his strand of advocacy. But even worse was the fact that something had gone so wrong with a galoi spaceship that they were contacting humans.

He protested the horror of that. "But this station is not one of those sanctioned to trade with Gal. If it were, I would not be here. We are light years from the nearest approved contact point."

His boss nodded. Her face was lined with the human version of concern. "Tris, I know this must be terrible for you, but we need your help. We are ill-prepared to parlay with the galoi and we don't want a galactic incident. Your people are touchy."

"At the best of times."

"Not you, of course."

Tris shrugged. Shrugging was a human trait that he had adopted. Mostly from close observation of Detective Hastion – Drey. The lovely detective made good use of shrugs and Tris found the gesture charmingly nonverbal. "I am *zyga,* formerly *loga*. It is my way to comfort. That ship coming toward us will be mostly *isoga*. A different type of communication will be required."

"You see? I have no idea what any of that means. None of us do. We need you desperately to sort this out for us."

"Will *you* be making the official greeting?"

"Unless you think you would be better?"

Tristol was often the face of outreach with alien ships, especially when the station was nervous about making contact. He was hard to rile, adapted easily to a range of cultural quirks and etiquette linguistics, and considered attractive by most bipedal humanoid species. Adjudicator Jones was not above using any of this to her diplomatic advantage, and neither was Tristol.

In this instance, however, he would be the wrong choice. "No, not me this time. You should do it or perhaps Ambassador Quinn."

His boss nodded. "If they ask for an in-person meet, will you be able to attend? Or would that be a cultural faux pas?"

"They will not ask. You will not be allowed on their ship and they would never set foot on a human space station." He took a tiny breath, then said before he lost his courage, "Why are they even approaching?" Tristol knew he had been working long enough with the adjudicator for her to see the worry in his hair.

"They seem to be in some kind of distress. Presumably we're the nearest station."

"Of course they have not told you the nature of that distress. That would show weakness. They will need to establish what the station's agenda might be first."

"We're willing to help!"

"Galoi do not believe in the existence of altruism. You must trade and barter hard. An *isoga* would rather die than ask for aid without balance. It is their role to bring unity and protection."

"But you are not like that at all."

Tristol nodded. "Exactly. *Loga* give of themselves and derive satisfaction in bringing comfort to others. Balance does not concern us. Which, so the legends say, is why we need union with an *isoga*, so we will not be exploited."

"But I thought you said your preference was for the other type?"

"*Antiga*? Yes. It is, as you humans might say, *kinky* of me not to be interested in both. Gal's most common unions are of three. The most highly regarded are of four: one *antiga*, one *loga,* and one of each *isoga*. I have only ever craved an *antiga*. This is considered a little perverted."

"Is that why you're in exile?"

"Detective Hastion asked the same thing recently. Interesting that the human mind instantly leaps to that. You place great significance on sexual orientation?"

"We did once. There have been bad times in our history regarding both sexual orientation and gender preferences."

"But you have settled into two?"

She made a funny sort of face. "Actually, no. Is that what you thought? The doctors will tell you that humans, mostly, are born with one of two possible biological sexes, but gender is more complicated."

Tris nodded. He found this part fascinating. Imagine, *from birth* to have a sexual identity! So strange. "With primary sexual organs in place. I know, amazing. And then you develop secondary sexual organs and characteristics and preferences during puberty? This has always seemed messy to me."

"Says the alien with five genders. There are exceptions, of course. And we make a distinction between biological sex and gender. Gender can be a matter of choice or instinct or both." She seemed to struggle for a moment. "A human may be born male and feel themself actually female, and vice versa. And there are some who prefer to exist in a liminal space between the two. They pick their pronouns accordingly. Recently the use of the dorien neutral has become popular."

Tris shook his head in wonder. "Yours is such a remarkably flexible species. Imagine switching one's gender! The idea is insane to my people." He frowned. "I would recommend not telling this to the galoi. There is a possibility they would reclassify humans as species-wide-psychotic and abort all communication everywhere, let alone trade."

Adjudicator Jones looked startled. "I will put out a diplomatic alert to that effect immediately. Thank you for saying something. It is not in our file on the galoi, so I suspect anthropologists don't know of this phobia."

Tris nodded. He did not think he had made a mistake in saying something, if it kept communication open. Yet he wondered if his people had the right to know that humans were, in fact, gender unstable. Then he remembered that the galoi were not actually *his* people anymore.

The supposition had been, before he left Gal, that humans were a binary species with fixed \*male\*female\* division and flexible sexual orientation. To find that this was not the case? He had to admit it rattled him. However, it did explain their ready acceptance and interbreeding with aliens like the dorien.

He tried to even conceive of it. Would he want, if he had the choice, to become *female*? Or to become *antiga* or *isoga*? He smiled at such whimsy. Alien indeed, to even entertain the thought. He was becoming almost human not to be utterly repulsed by it. Now who was being the flexible one? He decided to be pleased with himself.

Tris tried to explain the gravity of the taboo to his boss. "The dorien are considered, by the galoi, to be only one gender. The dorien, I understand, have made no effort to disabuse them of this notion."

"Smart."

Tris grinned. "Well, dorien have only one pronoun in their language, and they appear, outwardly, visually, the same. It is a fair assumption. They lack obvious sex characteristics."

The adjudicator grinned. "We call it *androgynous*. Some humans consider it very sexy." It was obviously something she herself found appealing, as one of her husbands was dorien – male-designated, but you'd never know that with his clothes on. "Tris, you've never before been so open with me about your people."

Tris nodded. "They are approaching. You will need to make informed decisions. And, of course, I do not know what you need explained, because to me it is all normal."

"Even after so long a time living among humans?"

"Even after. I thought I understood your genders, for example, and here you surprise me with their malleability. I thought there were two, now I find there are many. It is unsettling, my lack of knowledge. It is unfair of me to put you in the same position." Tris realized in this, too, he was being *loga*, providing knowledge to avoid discomfort. Everything, always, to avoid discomfort. "Although you will not be living among the galoi, so what you need to know is narrower in scope."

She nodded. "Given what I have told you so far about our current situation, which admittedly isn't much, what can you tell me?"

She was always very delicate concerning his *zyga* state. This was kind of her but also native to her role in society as an adjudicator. She imposed limits on her own curiosity in order to help others integrate. He very much appreciated it.

To be *zyga* meant not only becoming nothing to the galoi, but thinking nothing upon the galoi. He was supposed to forget. They were to be as meaningless to him as he was to them. It was like a state of profound atheism after holding for so long to a devout religious belief. He could question, he could intellectualize, and he could adapt to his new existence but not his old one. The galoi did not wish him dead. Of course they did not! All galoi were vested in the prevention of species extinction. But he no longer had meaning and neither did they. It was a complicated thing for a human to understand. To ask Tris to speak about, or even think on, his people was like asking him to perform a sermon within a temple to which he no longer belonged, concerning a faith he no longer believed.

Tristol was *zyga* and to be *zyga* was to be silent on matters galoi, because they were no longer his matters. Still, he was driven to help his humans now. He was still *loga* in the biological sense, and he supposed he might have to explain *that* little distinction to his boss at some point too. But for now, he scraped his mind for the most useful things, given their current predicament.

An unknown galoi ship, uncommunicative, yet approaching. The most likely explanation was that something had happened to the ship itself and that they needed to barter for repairs.

"Very well, adjudicator. Here is what I will say. No one will be allowed aboard. It does not matter the species." Tris wanted this clear. Humans were a curious race and they, as a rule, wanted to know everything about other aliens, particularly those to whom they had been denied access. Gal allowed no visitors. Gal sent forth no ambassadors. No galoi space stations or colonies permitted direct alien contact. Galoi were fierce in protection of their isolationist agenda.

Tris thought his species stupid in this. After all, what if they *could* crossbreed with humans? Their population problem might be fixed. Except, of course, that would cause impurities in the bloodlines. And what if they lost genders as a result?

Tris sighed. He was going to have to talk a lot more about his species than he wished. "Have there been any hints as to the nature of their distress?"

"Nothing at all. We've sent out an unmanned tug to pull them into dock. They've asked that the docking bay be clear of all living and inanimate portable objects. They were rather rude."

Tris nodded. "I am not trying to be cagey, my boss, but it would be best if we knew what they wanted before I gave any kind of instruction. And to whom. If someone does, by some small chance, need to go aboard, like a physician, then they will need different information than an ambassador or a mechanical engineer."

She nodded. "Yes, I see your point. This way you only have to repeat yourself once, to one team."

Tris grimaced. "I suppose Professor Frills will be present regardless?"

"It's his job, Tris."

Tristol's hair felt clammy and flat. Professor Frills was the station anthropologist and second cultural attaché. He had been trying to interview Tris for months. Since he first came aboard, in fact. As a private citizen of the station, Tristol had the right to refuse academic interview requests, which he did. But now it was a matter of station security, and Tris would have to tell people things about his culture. Professor Frills would be there in all his eagerness.

Tris did not think of Professor Frills so far as *human*male*enemy* but he was certainly not *human*male*friend*. The professor yearned so hard it was a stain around him. He looked at Tris with too much covetousness. Tristol's hair always got static in its effort to stick close to his own body. It was uncomfortable. Especially as Tristol was usually comfortable around *everyone*.

His boss took a fortifying breath. "Very well then, Tris, please, *please,* keep your com on you at all times. I'll ping you the moment we have further information and we'll go from there. It's likely Quinn will want you present when he opens communications. Off-screen, but present. That's *if* you think he'd be the best face for negotiations?"

Tris nodded. Ambassador Quinn was more aesthetically appealing than Adjudicator Jones. The human was all shades of medium brown, an attractive, uniform color that might encourage a modicum of improved communication with the galoi. But Tris did not want to have to say that to his boss. She might take offense.

"In that case, you're dismissed for the time being, but Tris, your con-com, please?"

"Yes, boss."

Tristol stood, grateful to escape. He felt a certain lightness to his hair, knowing he was now headed back to his detective, who was *waiting* for him. Who had said he would wait. Like a friend. Like perhaps even a *somate*. To pause one's life for another was a profound gesture of caring. *What greater gift can one give another person but time?*

Tris let himself fantasize. If Drey was his *somate...* (And he would use *Drey* in his head, because it was a name as pretty as the human himself)... If Drey was his *somate*, then Tristol would be going to Drey now for comfort. To be reassured and protected as an *isoga* might. To be loved and cherished as an *antiga* might. If Drey was his *somate,* would he hold Tris close? Would he press his bearded cheek to Tristol's smooth one in the caress of permanence?

Tris shook himself free of his fantasy, trying to fluff his hair to plump it up, make it sexy, eliminate thoughts of galoi ships and amorphous genders, and all other unexpected revelations. Knowing he must cope with them himself. Because it was silly to imagine one human might have capacity to be both *isoga* and *antiga*. It was even sillier for Tris to think, even if Drey could be all those things, that he would want to be them for Tristol Zyga.

Although Drey had said he would *wait*. And that gave Tris hope.

Drey waited for Tristol.

He told himself he was insane, that the cat was fine. (The cat was sleeping with a full belly and twitching whiskers. ) Drey had even, looking around furtively to ensure no one overheard, told Mister Montiguous that he was a *wonderful feline creature*.

He didn't need to stay in some strange couple's apartment and stare at a sleeping cat. Except Tris had seemed so thrilled that he might. It was oddly important to the galoi.

So Drey stayed.

He fiddled with his wrist-com, looking up articles on the galoi all over again. Wondering, as he always did, if he and Tris were compatible in their emotional needs. He had no doubt they would be compatible sexually, but he'd never heard of a galoi who liked being limited to one lover.

It was right there in the cultural anthropology article on his com:

*Field observation of* galoi *(zyga designation) among humans suggests that they are a sexually promiscuous species. Both males and females seem to prefer congress with species that show obviously male biological sex characteristics. We must assume, for procreative reasons, that there is another gender of galoi males who don't leave the planet, whose preferences is for females. Otherwise the species would die out.*

Drey snorted in amusement.

Imagine basing such an assumption on such a small sample size? There were perhaps one hundred galoi living among humans. Tris had said they were all *loga*, which was only one of the genders. Or maybe *loga* encompassed two genders? Still, one hundred, and this article thought it could understand an entire species? Even he knew that was flawed science, and Drey was no scientist.

He sighed and signaled his con-com into stasis.

Drey wandered around the living room. There was nothing there to help him understand Tris, as it wasn't Tristol's space. He wondered if it'd be okay to simply ask the galoi some of his many questions. Would his bright lavender boy consider monogamy, or was there some biological or emotional or cultural need for multiple lovers?

In this case, however, it might hurt to ask. Because what if the answer was yes? Then Drey would know forever that the most perfect creature he'd ever met couldn't be his to keep, only to share.

Drey didn't like sharing lovers.

He might consider it, though, for Tris.

Then he got mad at himself for even harboring the idea. He'd tried open relationships and polyamory in the past. It had hurt and ended badly.

So would it be better to ask and to know?

He picked up a funny carved animal from one of the living room shelves, turned it over in his hands.

Better not to know. Then he could cherish Tristol as a fantasy. Or was that fantasy too close to self-torture?

Drey sighed and made another circuit of the room.

He wished dispatch would call him in.

Except that would be a betrayal of Tris, who had asked him with such earnest hope if he would *wait*.

Drey sat back down and glared at the cat.

The cat slept on.

It seemed like ages, but eventually Tris returned.

His hair was flat, which worried Drey immediately. He jumped up. "What's wrong, honey?" *Whoops*.

Tris came over to him and his hair fluffed, reaching for him.

Drey loved that. He took it as a complement.

Tristol's smile was hopeful and he stopped slightly too close to Drey by human standards. "*Honey*? Like *honey*moon? Is that an endearment? Did you use an *endearment*? For me? And you waited. Thank you for waiting! But I have wondered, what does the excrement of an insect have to do with romantic relations? Not that I am not flattered."

"Excrement of an…" Drey tried to hide a smile. "Oh! *Honey* is a sweet-tasting syrup. It was once a popular condiment on Hu-Core. Highly valued. You know humans like the flavor of sweet things? Some even crave it."

Tristol tilted his head toward Drey, inquisitive expression, eager hair. He placed a tentative hand on Drey's arm again. This seemed to be a communicative gesture. "Would… you…" Tristol paused, uncertain. "Would you sit with me?"

Drey sighed and gave up a little. It couldn't be too

dangerous just to sit together, could it?

They sat next to each other on the small sofa. Tristol shifted toward him so they were in contact from shoulder to hip to leg. The galoi was cool, definitely cooler than human. A strand of his hair slid over, wrapped itself lovingly around Drey's neck. Like a silken scarf brushing sensually against him. Not grasping, yet not tentative, almost reassuring.

Drey tried not to like it.

Tristol's hair looked like lavender sunlight made solid. He wanted to touch and stroke but wasn't sure if that was allowed.

"Does it bother you?" Tris asked. "My hair? I can control it, if it bothers you."

There was such a wealth of yearning in the galoi's tone. Drey's own voice deepened in response. "No, it's comforting."

Tristol glowed as if he'd been praised. "And the endearment?"

Drey chuckled. "To be called anything sweet by a human, in general, is a compliment. It just slipped out. I meant no insult."

"None taken! You may call me *honey* whenever you wish. Although it is not the right color for me, is it?"

"True. Honey is not purple."

Tris blinked at him. "I am *lavender*!"

Drey tried to hide a smile, "Lavender is a type of purple."

"I know that. I memorized all the shades. But *lavender* is more accurate and it is a superior word." The alien seemed very set on this point. "Is there a sweet human treat that is lavender colored?"

"Not one commonly used as an endearment. Taro root perhaps. Or grape candy."

Tristol shook his head. "Those words are too harsh. I prefer *honey*."

Drey said, despite himself, "Grape candy is my favorite."

"You like sweet things?"

"I do. Do the galoi use endearments?"

Tris shook his head. "Not really. Not words that mean other words. Elle calls her Olav *husband* as a term of affection. *Come here, husband*, she will say. We might do something like that."

Drey felt out of his depth and tentative and desperate. "Perhaps not exactly what I mean to ask. *Husband* is more permanent, it has social and legal implications. My question was more... Please, never feel you must answer my questions, if speaking of such things is rude, or taboo, or makes you uncomfortable."

The hair didn't stop its soft caresses.

"Oh, detective. I do not mind with you. I should like you to understand me better. I may be *zyga* but I was raised galoi. As I have only recently learned, adapting is not so easy on either side. May I ask you questions also that may be rude or intrusive? And you could extend me the same courtesy of silence rather than offense?"

Drey winced but nodded. This was dangerous territory, but it was also a chance at insight. "Do you have the concept of husband then?"

Tristol's hair stilled a moment, then resumed caressing. "We have something similar to your concept of *spouse,* but there is no gendered term like *husband* or *wife*. Our idea of spousal contracts seems similar to yours. It is a lover or lovers with whom you choose to stay. Galoi interpret spouse as the *home*color*foundation* of your soul. A mate of the heart rather than the body, although often also *as well as* the body." His big eyes managed to look sultry.

*He's such a flirt.* Still the words gave Drey hope. "Marriage?" Drey couldn't stop the swell of yearning. "Exclusive marriage?"

"Sometimes, yes. We call the union itself *mycota*. But it translates well enough to the human idea of marriage. A galoi *mycota* can be two or more individuals. But for us it is never of the same gender, never more than four, and never for the purposes of procreation."

Drey blinked. There was so much to unpack there. Did Tristol, for example, think of him, Drey, as the same gender and thus taboo for marriage? But more startlingly, "Galoi don't have children?"

Tris gave one of his melodic trills of amusement and his hair shook. "Of course we have younglings! But not within a *mycota*. That is what *gamein* is for."

Drey puffed out his lips. "Okay?"

Tris seemed game and kept explaining. "*Gamein* is a breeding union between two individuals for the purposes of procreation only, and therefore only exists between *antiga* and *loga*."

"And who takes care of the resulting, uh, results?"

"Offspring are given into care of *isoga* who rear them as an age group. I think you might call this a creche?"

"You don't raise your own children?"

"We do not."

"Have you had children, Tris?"

Tristol's hair instantly flattened. This, apparently, was not a safe question.

Drey hastily backpedaled. "Forget I asked. Let's go back to sex?"

"Yes please!" The hair resumed petting. Tris seemed to feel this was an opening to ask his own question. "If I give you the right answers, would you perhaps, consider sex with me? You are interested in male genitalia?"

Drey smiled. "I'm gay, yes."

"And you find me appealing?"

"Doesn't everyone?"

"No. But thank you for the compliment. Until today, I would have said a certain detective was immune to my charms."

"That would be a total lie." Drey couldn't have him

think such a thing. "Did your hair just *wiggle*?"

Tris dipped his head, eyes lowered. "Yes. I find you very attractive, Detective Drey Hastion." He gave another little trill at the end of the sentence, almost sub-vocal. Perhaps those non-word noises were a kind of galoi endearment.

Drey responded with, "It's mutual."

He took his courage in hand, then, and asked the question he most feared, hoping he was phrasing things properly. "Those who don't have a spouse, like you, what do you call the people you sleep with? You've lovers, I've seen it." Drey winced at the memory. "Is there a name for that?"

"It would be a direct translation, I suspect. *Lovers* works well enough."

Drey tried again. "And are all galoi looking for a spouse? Or, um, spouses?"

Tristol looked thoughtful. "Not all. Of course, people's preferences vary widely. Most galoi look for two others, some yearn for all possible. I have only ever wished for an *antiga*. Now, of course, that is not possible for me."

Drey could feel his shoulders sag. So there was his answer. Tris liked, or needed, to play the field.

Tris shifted as if sensing his disappointment. "I have injured you with my words. What did I say that was wrong? I assure you lack of *antiga* is no great hardship, if your concern is there. Human males have, mostly, once I learned the correct terms for what I require sexually, proven to be excellent lovers. You are not entirely the same genital configuration as an *antiga*, of course, but you are good at fucking! I mean humans must be, there are so many of you."

Drey couldn't help his chuckle at that. "True that."

"Then what did I say that made you sad?"

"I suppose I meant to ask, without the possibility of an *antiga*, whether your preference is for many lovers." Drey tried not to hold his breath, waiting for the inevitable crushing disappointment.

Tristol's hair wilted and he said something Drey would never have expected. "None of them have wanted me to \*stay\*home\*future\*keep\*." Tris ran his terms together sometimes when he couldn't find the right word in galactic standard, as if he thought all of them together must be more precise or that the union of the words changed their overall meaning.

*Bullshit.* Who wouldn't want such a man for more than one night? Humans could be remarkably stupid, Drey wasn't the first to say that, but they weren't *that* stupid.

He frowned, thinking about the dynamics of gay clubs and one-night stands. "Did you ask for a second date?"

Tris looked up, startled. "I could do that?"

"Of course."

Tris brightened considerably. "If we had sex, you and I, would you like a second date? May I ask you now or is that rude? You did wait here for me. You offered up your time, which does me great honor. You continue to give it to me now, so generously, as if you were a *loga* yourself. I…"

He trailed off. "I am doing this wrong again. We may not be compatible. I should at least ask that first. Shouldn't I? Or is that also wrong? Have I been doing it all badly and backward? Have I offended my lovers by not asking? Have I been inconsiderate? Was I supposed to keep *them*?"

Drey could only blink in surprise as the galoi wound himself up into a panic. He tried to interrupt but Tristol kept talking.

"Were they emotionally hurt? Was I wrong not to ask? We *loga*, we are always asked. Because we are those who caretake, who give and paint the nest, so it is assumed we would like to be kept and thus it is the other partner's responsibility to make the request. If unasked, the *loga* assumes they are free to try another."

Drey frowned. "Okay there, calm down. You've done nothing wrong. One-night stands are common among humans. It's considered normal to experiment, and try out a prospective partner sexually. Then you ask for more. If you wish to sleep together again or if you wish to date. Dating means more companionship than just sex. Sometimes it implies that there is the possibility of a spousal contract. But dating doesn't necessarily guarantee that. Communication of preferences and intent is important. Does that make sense?"

Tristol let out a breath. "I think so."

"But you were waiting to be asked, because you're *loga*?" Drey had a sudden horrible feeling that all the gay men he'd seen leaving with Tristol over the months had been taking advantage of the young man.

Tris nodded. "Yes, exactly. Although I did not *want* to stay with them. I should still have liked to be asked."

"They treated you well? They did nothing to hurt you emotionally or physically?" Had this lovely creature been inadvertently abused?

Tris squeezed the hand he'd rested on Drey's arm, warm and reassuring and carefully placed above the cat scratches. "Oh, no! It was fun. Not very flattering that they did not want me more or again or for any length of time, but now I see that is not a flaw in me. I thought maybe, to you humans, I was – how do you put it? *Bad in bed*."

Drey bristled. "In the clubs, afterward, did any of them flirt with you again?"

Tristol nodded. "Yes. And I always thought it very odd. I mean if they did not like me, why try again? I thought perhaps it was a kind of compliment, to help me, you know, so others would not know I had been found wanting."

Drey almost felt like crying. *Poor baby!*

Tris continued. "But had they asked to keep me I would have said no, anyway."

Which brought them right back to the source of all Drey's worry. "What do you want then, in the end?"

Tris looked at him like he was insane. "I want *you* to keep me, of course."

# THE 4<sup>TH</sup> CHAPTER

## *Five gender foreplay*

Tris thought he should be very clear to prevent further confusion on the part of this lovely human. So he added, "That is, assuming we are compatible in the manner of gay humans."

Drey managed to look both flattered, and horrified, and embarrassed, and delighted, all at the same time. It was very pretty on him.

Drey had also stopped talking and had his mouth open slightly.

Tris felt perhaps this meant it was his turn to ask questions. Luckily, he had learned some of this part of *human*male*gay* interaction. The part that was all about articulating sexual preference.

This negotiation was customarily done during the initial stage of *human*club*courtship*. It included ritualized dancing and plumage displays, like face paint and shirt slogans. But Tris had never danced with Drey. Drey only came to the clubs to watch and to drink with friends. It occurred to Tris to worry, for the first time, that they may not be physically compatible.

This was a concern that must be dealt with immediately.

"I am a bottom!" Tristol blurted out. His hair almost spiked up due to the riot of emotions flowing through him.

Drey stroked his hair, gently. Humans never realized

what an intimate act that was. Yet with Drey, Tris loved it. Drey's massive warm hands threading through his agitated locks were both arousing and comforting.

"Okay, Tris. That's fine." Drey's eyes looked *happy* friendly*sexy*. Perhaps he was considering calling Tristol *honey* again?

"You are a *top*, right?"

Drey smiled. "I'm versatile, but I like topping very much and if that's your preference…"

Tris decided to get very serious, only partly aware that he had climbed into the big human's lap so he might take that lovely bearded face into his hands and focus Drey's full attention on his own earnestness.

"*Loga* do not climax without penetration. *Male loga* are what humans would call *bottoms* but it is by biological necessity as well as choice. *Female loga* are the same."

"But you have a cock?" Drey was clearly confused.

Tristol's penis had been hard and seeping since they sat down on the couch together. Now that he had this human in his arms and under him, it was only becoming more so. Tris demonstrated its existence by grinding against the detective's flat stomach.

"Yes, I am male." Tristol did not bother to explain that the term male only applied to his external organs and overall appearance, because in the past this had upset his human lovers. It did not matter. A human could never drive him into estrus and get him pregnant. Drey need not know he had all the necessary equipment to conceive young. That was, after all, his burden and his sacrifice. The reason for his exile, refusal of *gamein*, a *loga's* greatest sin.

Drey had said he was *versatile* so Tristol added, hastily, "I would be happy to try to penetrate you, but I am unable to achieve orgasm that way."

Drey only kept smiling.

Tris relaxed. "That is good?"

"You only get off if I fuck you into the mattress? Yeah,

that's good. That's great. Wanna try?" Drey arched up under him.

Tris was both pleased and surprised by the size of the penis pressing against his wiggling ass.

He squeaked. "Here? I do not think that is proper. And Mister Montiguous might see! Or be disturbed."

"So come back with me to my quarters. And if you'll maybe think about me keeping you, or you keeping me, I don't care which, I'll show you what a good top I can be."

Tris could not suppress his little trill of pleasure at that idea. This was perhaps the best thing *ever*. A human male was considering him, Tristol Zyga, as a *somate*. Or as close as humans got. A human was entertaining the possibility of a future together. And not just any human, but his *human*male*favorite*wishwishwish*, whom Tris had thought aloof or at least disinterested. Apparently, all Tris had ever needed to do was state his wish to be kept. That he would be fine with just one spouse for as long as such a thing lasted among humans. With Drey!

"Now?" he said hopefully.

Drey chuckled. "Yes. Now. Although I think we're both on con-com reserve."

Tristol got serious and nodded.

Drey's big warm hands began to stroke over his back. As Tris had been instructed to stroke Mister Montiguous. He liked it so much. He understood the appeal now. He wondered if he too should purr. But he was not *isoga*, so he did not really have the sub-vocal range.

"I'll not ask you why, Tris, because I'm sure it's a need-to-know basis."

Tris was pleased that Drey respected the delicacy of his job, but he did say, "I do hope you never need to know."

Because if the incoming galoi ship required Drey in his official capacity as a member of security, that meant violence, which was no good thing for anyone.

Drey obviously understood. "Me too, Tris. Me too."

Tris sighed and allowed himself the luxury of pressing every part of himself against Drey's big warm body, this human he wanted so very badly. The hardness of him, the size – so much size! He nuzzled against the roughness of beard, the possibility of permanence. He let his hair do as it willed, caressing and drifting about them, reaching also for this human.

And all he could think was: *Oh please decide to keep me. When this night is over, ask me to stay. If only for a little while. Ask me to do human dating things.* Tristol had no deity but the universe, so he sent his begging toward the stars. *Please ensure this* galoi *ship not mess everything up. Please do not let others break into this dream. I would like this human to be mine. I would be so good to him. I would cherish so hard. I would be the best* loga *ever. I would be the best \*human\*spouse\*creature\* ever, for him.*

"Mister Montiguous is watching," whispered Drey. Though his hands kept stroking Tristol's back.

"Your quarters, then?"

Drey stood, still holding Tris wrapped around him. Drey's arms bulged but he kept Tris cradled easily. Big hands slid down to support Tristol's ass, they curved a little, explored. Tris squirmed happily, settling into the grip. Drey gave a lovely low groan.

"Mmmhmm, but I'll have to set you down. I can't walk though a space station carrying you. Fun as that'd be. I mean, I could, but as I'm a detective on the security force, that's a bit unprofessional. And it's a bit out of character."

"You're right. Mrs Ullriche would probably see, and then ask questions, and then talk to *everyone* about it."

Drey gently set Tristol down. Tris stayed close the whole time, sliding against Drey's body and trilling with the pleasure of it, so warm and hard.

Drey shuddered, stepped away, and took a shaky breath. "Mrs Ullriche is a gossip?"

"If that word means she will make up stories about you

if you are not interesting enough to start with, then yes."

"But you're still nice to her?"

"Her stories are fun, when they are not about me."

Drey put a hand to his heart and fluttered his eyelashes. "Why Mr Tristol, are you telling me that you too are a gossip?"

"Is that bad?"

"Only if you refuse to tell me what she says."

Tristol thought this might be Drey's version of the human's much maligned *sense of humor*. Tris was being *teased*, perhaps?

He tried his own version. "But then I should be the gossip? And how would that look? A socially upstanding alien like myself."

Drey chuckled, so Tris had executed the tease correctly. Tristol's hair wiggled happily.

Drey took Tristol's hand then, which was wonderful! This was a human sign of fixed affection permitted in public. It was not as nice as being carried wrapped around Drey, but it would do for now.

Drey held Tristol's cool hand in his own. The galoi's grip was firm and dry. His hand was small and slender but strong. His nails were white and round, looking almost human. But Drey supposed, given that Tristol's teeth were white too, and parts of his big eyes, that not everything was purple. Or, erm, *lavender*.

Drey liked being seen with Tris.

Let them gossip.

He lived in Zone 3 too, of course.

He was a little embarrassed by his quarters, as he let Tristol inside. Looking at his living room through the eyes of an alien, he realized how sparse and unfriendly it appeared.

"Sorry it's so bare. I don't spend much time at home."

There was no reason. No one was ever waiting for him. Perhaps that was the kind of waiting that had made Tris so happy. The presence of another that was not just time and attention but a balm for loneliness. He wondered, being galoi, what Tristol's quarters looked like, and wished they'd gone there instead.

Tris looked around with bright eyes, not letting go of Drey's hand.

"You do not collect the things for walls and shelves like other humans?"

"No, I'm rather spartan."

"A good word, I think. But galoi tend to be *spartan* too, then. Although we like pillows a lot."

Drey didn't know what to say to that offered-up tidbit, so he only nodded. He supposed he could get behind a nice pillow or two. Or on top of. Or draped over.

"Would you like to come through to the bedroom?"

Tristol gave a funny little start. His hair fluttered. "Oh yes, of course. I forget sometimes."

"Forget what, baby?"

"That you designate your rooms."

Drey thought this was likely not particularly important at the moment. If and when he saw Tristol's quarters he'd understand, so he let it drop.

"Drey, *baby* is another endearment, yes?"

"Yeah, that's okay?" Drey felt his face heat. He was moving too fast, probably. He did that sometimes. Wanted too much, too quickly. It's one of the reasons he held himself back from relationships, stiff and prickly. Grumpy, Tris had called him.

"*Baby* is not an odd word? Your younglings are sexually taboo, are they not?"

"Of course!" Drey had never considered it. And now he was ashamed to have used the endearment, it just slipped out... again.

A slim lavender hand came up, pressed Drey's chin so

he must look into Tristol's big eyes. "Drey, I like it. I've heard human lovers use it on each other. *Please* call me *baby*."

Drey looked away from those hopeful purple eyes, but nodded. Of course he would call Tris that. He would call Tris anything Tris wanted. *Snuggle-bottom-tentacle-head* if he liked.

Drey started leading Tris toward his bed when both of their coms went off. Tristol's flashed. Drey's blared into his ear.

"Well fuck, that's my com too."

Tristol's hair flattened. "They want us both?"

Drey nodded. "Not a good sign."

Tris picked up his unit. "Yes, adjudicator?"

Drey engaged his own ear-com. "Yes?"

Dispatch said, sharp and curt, "Report in person to security ops for a briefing."

"Shit," said Drey.

"Exactly," agreed dispatch.

He tapped it off and looked at Tris, whose eyes were wide and hair was flat.

"Security ops?" said Drey.

Tris nodded. "Me too."

"Trouble?"

Tris nodded again. "Indubitably."

Drey did love his big words. It was adorable.

Tris hated that Drey had been called in with him. Not that he objected to more time spent with the detective, just that it meant there was something criminal going on with the galoi ship.

Drey did not hold his hand this time as they walked toward the grav-free hub. They hit the transport without breaking stride, both pushing off to float toward Zone 1. It was delineated by a red light, blinking at a steady interval, and, for those who required other senses, a subtle scent distinguished it from others (which Tris couldn't smell, as galoi didn't have sensitive noses). There was also a unique texture to the walls. Each zone was different, a rainbow of lights at the inner core which Tris found quite pretty. Zone 3, disappearing behind them, was yellow, bright and cheerful, the lights blinking three fast and then a long pause, before three again.

Security had their operation center in Zone 1, and their communication hub in Zone 6, both at station edge, and essentially polar opposites. Tris understood this reasoning. If one part of the station were damaged, ideally the other half of security would remain functioning and autonomous.

He and Drey were the last to arrive, but no one gave them funny looks for doing so together. Tristol thought they might have, if Drey held his hand. His fingers twitched, too cold without the firm comfort of the detective's warm touch.

"Detective Hastion, Mr Zyga, how nice of you to join us."

Tris thought that was sarcasm in the Station Master's tone. He still struggled to identify human sarcasm, and couldn't simulate it at all himself.

Master Crisolla was young for xer job, or xe *looked* young. Xer hair was black like Drey's but not curly at all – instead it was straight and thick and cut sharp. Tris shivered at the idea of cutting hair. When it was chopped to mid-length like the station master's, it looked painful to him. Short was utterly alien, and long was completely familiar, but mid-length and blunt? Cruel.

Master Crisolla's skin was not as dark as Drey's and xer eyes were augmented – impossible to tell what color they started as, with the micro-crystalline segmentation that allowed xer access to all ranges of light and motion and distance.

Galoi did not engage in surgical modification except in cases of injury. Tristol found, when it was functional, as with the station master, that he could sympathize, but aesthetic augmentations for purely cosmetic reasons? Those he found disturbing. Except piercings, of course. He supposed he would learn to get over the other kind eventually.

Their Chief of Security, Drey's boss, was one of those pale pink humans. She wore her orange hair short and had small orange spots all over her face. This, Tris now knew, was a natural recessive human coloration. He found it fascinating. He'd copulated with a human male once with similar speckles and tried to lick all the spots. The male in question had not appreciated the attention. The chief also had an aesthetic augmentation of colorful art painted all over her arms, and presumably other parts of her body. Tattoos, they were called. Tris found them both fascinating for their bright beauty, and repugnant for their permanent state of skin scarring. But he had learned not to shudder at the sight.

He wondered if there was something about galoi appearance that accidentally caused a visceral reaction in humans. Earrings for decoration seemed almost ubiquitous among humans, so those were unlikely to traumatize. But was there some other thing his people did that inadvertently disturbed humans? The wiggling hair, perhaps?

"Sit, those who wish to, and let's begin the briefing." Master Crisolla was all business, all the time. Xe had never offered to socialize with Tris, and he did not even know xer first name.

Drey took an empty seat to one side.

Tris decided to remain standing. The only other empty chair was next to Professor Frills and that location did not appeal.

An image flashed in the vid before them. It was an achingly familiar scene. The bridge of a galoi ship.

Only one *isoga* was visible, taking up most of the view

field, intentionally, of course. They would not want the humans to know how many manned their bridge.

"A little over an hour ago we received an audio-only hail from a galoi ship requesting to dock. Here." Master Crisolla looked around, or seemed to look around – difficult to tell with eye-augs.

Whatever xe saw satisfied xer.

Everyone in that room was suitably awed and understood the unprecedented nature of such contact.

"We sent an unmanned tug to guide them in. They did not require mechanical assistance. Once docked, they initiated contact with us visually. This has never before occurred with a galoi ship. Ever. Even trade negotiations are conducted only in audio, and goods are exchanged via drone between ships."

"Why visual contact then?" asked Adjudicator Jones, looking between the station master, the vid, and Tris – as if Tris knew what was going on.

"They are requesting the aid of a neutral party, a human criminal investigator."

Now everyone turned to look at Drey. There were other members of station security, of course, but Drey was their only detective qualified to investigate major crimes.

"Me?" The big human looked startled, then he too looked at Tris.

The station master continued. "There's been a murder on the galoi ship."

Tris shook his head and spoke, so startled as to be rude in the face of his superiors. "Not possible."

Master Crisolla looked at him. "I assure you, there's no mistake in translation."

Tris could feel his hair tremble in agitation. "There must be a mistake. Galoi do not kill each other."

"Never?"

"Never. We have no word for *murder*. We make war, but only defensively against *other* species."

Master Crisolla cocked xer head. "It's true the word *murder* didn't seem to exist in the vid. The exact phrasing the galoi used was that *a life had been taken, not by accident*."

Tris was gobsmacked. *Gobsmacked* being a much superior word to *murder*. "But that does not happen."

"Never?"

"Not to my knowledge or education. What purpose could it possibly serve?'

The humans all looked at one another.

Tris continued to not believe. "How is it possible?"

"This is why we've been contacted. Apparently, the galoi don't know how to find a murderer."

Tris nodded, then looked at Drey. "There is no need for such a role as detective in galoi culture." He explained for Drey alone, although everyone else listened. "We have no murder, theft, or rape. We do not kill each other. We do not keep personal possessions for others to steal."

"No crime at all?" Drey was flabbergasted.

Tris frowned. "Not as humans understand it. There are crimes of etiquette and reproductive choice. There are breaches in professional roles or gender duty. But it is rarely mysterious as to who is the cause. And, of course, for the worst offense there is only one punishment."

"Exile." Drey said it as he stared at Tris, hard.

Tris said to him, loud enough for the others to hear. "Yes."

Drey looked sick. "You're a criminal, Tris?" It was whispered.

"No, not as humans think it." Tristol ached to touch him, to comfort and be comforted, but he remained standing and apart. "*Zyga* are nothing at all. We do not fit. You might call us, perhaps, aberrant? It is through our own choice that we are rejected. There is no space for us as galoi. No time can be given to a *loga* who does not do their duty. But ours is a choice that does not harm another person, physically or mentally. I swear it. A *zyga* has harmed the greater good of all galoi through denial, but that is all."

The station master was distracted by the possibility that Tris was a danger to xer station. "Treason?" she barked.

Tris shook his head, frustrated. "No. *Zyga* is not the result of something humans would see as a crime."

"You're sure of this?"

Tris nodded emphatically. "Positive."

"What did you do, Tris?" Drey asked.

"It is not relevant. Please believe me. It will have no bearing on the humans I interact with, on human or other alien cultures, or on my job performance. Also please believe me when I say that among galoi, murder is not possible."

"You don't have psychopaths?" That was Drey again. He seemed to have decided to believe Tris. Although Tristol thought he was likely to be interrogated more on the subject later. But for now, Drey's mind was already working on the mystery presented to him:

A species that had no word for *murder* had a murderer aboard their ship.

Tris gave the concept of *psychopath* serious thought. He had read about the condition when studying humans. "Violent aggression combined with an inability to socialize or empathize? No. We do not have that."

Master Crisolla put a stop to Drey's need to begin investigating immediately. "Regardless, we must look at the facts. A ship full of an unknown number of galoi has docked here on my station because they need a murder solved." Xe directed everyone's attention back to the vid.

The galoi spoke his native tongue into the vid-com. The space station's translator dubbed over the words, so that the voice and mouth movements did not match. This was a common tactic, but Tristol found it unsettling when applied to his own species. He could not read the nuances in the vocabulary.

They listened to what amounted to a short but brief opening salvo in a trade negotiation. It made sense to Tris. There was no way a galoi would make a request of another species for aid, not even in this matter – it must be a trade.

"Humans of Space Station XO17, this galoi ship, the *Winds of Constancy*, would barter for the services of a human detective. We have an involuntary non-accidental death aboard our ship. We must know why. What would you trade for this service?"

# The 5<sup>th</sup> Chapter

## *Embattled briefing*

Drey couldn't process what Tris had said about the reasons for his exile, so he put it aside. For now, he hoped it had no relevance to the case at hand.

The situation seemed oddly clear when looking at the facts independent of galoi culture.

A murder on a spaceship.

Drey liked the odds. It meant a set number of possible culprits. None of whom were likely to be career criminals or serial killers, which meant they were not trained to hide their tracks.

Even considering the nuances of alien culture, it should be relatively simple to find the killer. In fact, it was just the kind of case Drey liked best.

"Tris," – he stopped himself – "Mr Zyga, how many galoi are likely to be aboard this ship?"

Tristol, oddly, held up a hand to stop him from talking. It was a very un-Tris gesture. He was not a particularly commanding presence although he'd obviously learned that move from the station master. He even imitated xer posture when he did it.

"A moment, Detective Hastion. Please, Master of Station, may I hear the galoi words as spoken originally in the home tongue?"

Master Crisolla was disposed to find this a waste of

time. "It's already been translated."

Professor Frills added, "I checked over the work myself. It's an excellent translation."

Tristol remained stubborn. "All apologizes, but I must insist. The nuances are missing. Please?"

The station master sniffed and then gestured curtly to her tech aid in the corner, who made some few adjustments and then played back the recording without the dubbing.

Drey thought the galoi language sounded beautiful, lyrical, and melodic. So did many of the others in the room, apparently, as most could not keep from smiling.

Tristol, who was not smiling for a change, held up his hand again. The tech paused the recording.

Tris said, slowly, clearly concentrating on his own version of translation. "The vid's mandate is directed only to humans. Thus it would be a grave insult to involve any other species in any part of this negotiation. That includes those only part-human. Also those who might *appear* to be only part human." Tris looked at the security chief. "One could suppose, for example, that your tattoos could be caused by a cross-contamination birth. As might your eyes, Master Crisolla. I recommend visual contact only with those who are as close to human birth-state as possible." He looked at his own boss. "Adjudicator, I believe your hair will be fine."

Adjudicator Jones barked out a surprised laugh. "You knew I dyed it?"

Tris blinked at her. "Of course. Others do not?"

Professor Frills was coding frantically into his com, eyes avid on Tristol's face. He was clearly hypnotized by every nugget of insight Tris provided. Occasionally, he licked his lips in a kind of avarice that Drey found disturbing.

Drey had never liked Professor Frills. Now he decided that he hated him.

Tris nodded to the tech and more lilting galoi permeated the room until Tris held up his hand again.

"*Winds of Constancy* is not right."

Frills opened his mouth to object and then snapped it shut.

Tris was thinking hard. "Perhaps *Reliability of a Steady Wind?*"

"Who cares what their ship is called?" Master Crisolla was losing xer patience.

"Master of Station!" Drey had never seen Tris look so stern. "*All* names have meaning and import. *All of them.* Meaning is power." He gestured to himself. "In naming me *zyga,* my people stripped me of social identity and rendered me powerless. This galoi ship has a name that finishes in an *aaaaee* sound." Tris made the noise, ending it with a slight click. "This tells us that the captain of this ship, as humans might call him, is *antiga.* This is rare but not unheard of. *Antiga* do not usually leave Gal. The man on the vid, however, is *isoga.*"

"That means what, exactly?" Adjudicator Jones was accustomed to dealing with Tristol and her tone was gentle and encouraging.

Tris looked frustrated. "For galoi, everything is in name and gender. *Everything.* Name and gender are one, united. This station" – he made an encompassing gesture with one hand – "*we* were snubbed subtly by this vid. An *antiga* captain, but an *isoga* communicating with us? That is an insult, to us, to humans. It is not a grave insult, but it is significant that the trade negotiation was not opened by the captain himself. You may take offense or not, station master, but please know that you have been given offense. Now, play the next section please."

He listened, then stopped playback again. "The barter for Drey's services is only for that, thank goodness, and not for Drey himself."

Drey felt his scalp prickle.

"You keep *slaves*?" Master Crisolla was truly horrified by that.

Tris seemed to find her shock amusing. His hair-tips twitched. "No. The word for barter has multiple meanings depending on context, particularly when applied to a person and his abilities. Drey is a fertile male, or I assume he is fertile, and there is a possibility, however small, that if his intelligence were greatly admired, the ship would barter for both his skills as a detective and his genetic material for scientific study. Fertility is of great interest to the galoi. In this instance, however, you will be pleased to know, Detective Hastion, that they are only interested in your mind and not your sperm."

Drey was indeed relieved.

Tris looked hard at the station master and at then at his own boss. "This is why you must not agree to *any* trade that has not been carefully vetted."

Master Crisolla was finally taking Tris seriously. "I see."

Everyone in the room let out a collective breath.

"Play some more, please?" Tris gave the aide a little apology smile for all his hard work.

Soon enough, he had him pause yet again. "This part was translated well." He nodded to Professor Frills, a better diplomat than Drey would have been under the circumstances.

Drey's lip curled and he wanted Tris to look at him.

Tristol's eyes went unfocused, clearly sad and traumatized by what he must say next. His hair lay flat and limp. Then he looked at Drey. "Your *murder victim* is a *male loga*. You can tell by the ending of the word used for *dead individual*. Modifiers, verbs, and pronouns are conjugated for each gender. Similarly, the insistence on knowing why and what exactly happened is coming from the *antiga* captain, not from Gal. This spaceship may, or may not, have planetary backing for this trade."

Master Crisolla paled. "So this could become a diplomatic incident? What are the pitfalls, ambassador, in either case?"

Ambassador Quinn, who'd been sitting in silent

concentration, frowned. "If the ship's approach is sanctioned by the home planet, this contact, or *trade* as Mr Zyga insists we call it, could be seen as possible outreach, furthering inter-species relations." He looked at Tris for support.

Tris nodded. "You may think of it that way, Ambassador, if it makes you feel good."

Ambassador Quinn continued. "If the *antiga* captain is approaching us privately, I honestly don't know. All trades with galoi until now have been under Gal's approval. The nuances of the power structures and politics of Gal are unknown." He looked at Tris again. "Is this captain likely to represent only his ship, only himself, or some larger galoi political faction?"

Tris shrugged. "I can not tell. Ours is a nuanced language, ambassador, but not nuanced enough to fathom the nature of intent. There is a saying on Gal that would translate something like: *words lie but the truth is in the hair.*"

Everyone stared at him.

Drey thought he understood a bit more than anyone else did, even Professor Frills. After all, he was achingly familiar with Tristol's amazing hair.

Tris asked the aide to play the last bit of the vid.

Into the silence following it, he said, "The last line formally requests a trade. It should be familiar to any who have traded with galoi before. It is always the same wording. There is no conjugation to *service* because they do not know Drey's gender, so it is left plural, although demoted-plural to indicate only one. In other words, they want only *a single detective* to board. You will have to send Detective Hastion in alone."

Drey could feel his heart sink. "But I've no diplomatic training to infiltrate an alien spaceship!" he said, realizing that he was talking at the same time as a number of others in the room.

A mild chaos ensued while everyone protested. Drey's boss didn't like sending in a man without backup. Professor Frills wanted more than anything to get onto that spaceship. The ambassador thought it very ill-advised to send anyone without training, and so forth.

Tris, Drey noticed after he got hold of his own panic, only stood and watched everyone's reactions. His hair vibrated with interest.

Finally, they all quieted and the adjudicator asked her employee, "Tris, is there a way we could barter to have you join Detective Hastion on the ship? At least that would give us some kind of insight and help him acclimatize."

Tristol gave a semi-evil smile. "Ah, now *that* is a good question, *human*female*boss*. I believe that I could simply accompany the detective. Since I am *zyga*, I cannot be part of a trade, but also, I cannot be acknowledged as existing at all." Purple eyes turned on Drey.

Drey smiled back a little evilly back. "Essentially, since to them you are nothing, then you can come with me and they can't or won't acknowledge your presence? Also you wouldn't apply to the verbal insistence on a single person boarding."

Tris nodded. "It is a risk, of course. If they decide to somehow take insult, it could cause an intergalactic incident. But it is a very small risk, especially with an *antiga* captain."

"What does that mean?" asked Professor Frills.

Tristol only said, "It might be argued that someone like me, who once wore the black ring, is more significant to *antiga* than any other gender. I am more of an insult to the first gender because I choose exile, so even less worthy of acknowledgement."

"Black ring? I don't understand. You mean the earrings? We have always wondered, what do they mean?" That was Professor Frills, of course. He explained to the others, pedantically, "The non-exile galoi all wear rings in the right ear of varying number and color, and sometimes studs in the left ear, of similar colors. Speculation is that it's a ranking system."

"How do you know about the earrings?" Tristol's beautiful pointed ears were barren. Although Drey had noticed he had a hole in his right one.

Professor Frills looked smug. "We know more about the galoi than the galoi think we do."

"Apparently not enough to translate our language sufficiently," snapped back Tris.

Professor Frills was undaunted. "So what do the earrings mean?"

Tris waggled a hand in the air. "It does not matter, professor. What matters is we might get away with me accompanying the detective aboard. It would be helpful, as I can interpret all the nuances of language and culture that your computer translator will miss."

Drey spoke before Professor Frills could continue being nosy. "We'd be using their rejection of you against them? I like it." And Drey did. He really wanted to punish the galoi for being cruel to this lovely man.

Tristol's hair deflated. "You misunderstand, detective. The galoi did not reject me, I rejected them. But that is irrelevant because either way this might still work. I am sorry, though," he spoke firmly to the dignitaries assembled, particularly the professor, "but there will be absolutely no way to add anyone else to the boarding party. The trade was opened with a request for only one person. Entering the barter means you must accept those initial terms. The loophole is that I am no longer a person. Only I qualify as that."

And off they went, discussing whether they could rig Drey or Tris or both up with recording devices, and what other aspects of the negotiation might be fiddled with.

Drey paid attention but only with half of his brain. The other half was busy both calculating investigation tactics and panicking over the fact that he was about to be the first human ever to visit a galoi ship.

He watched Tris out of the corner of his eye. The young man's hair was getting agitated and finally, during a lull in the discussion, he spoke up.

"I am so sorry, station master, but there is more to the vid that I have not explained."

"More?"

Tris winced. "You see why *zyga* do not often discuss galoi with anthropologists like Professor Frills? It is overly detailed. But in this case, there is still something important that your translator missed."

Professor Frills snorted softly. Hard to know if that was self-criticism or general annoyance at his own lack of understanding.

Adjudicator Jones glared at the anthropologist. "You have been immensely helpful so far, Tristol. By all means, what else?"

Master Crisolla looked frustrated but resigned.

Tris gave another smile. This one was forced and not genuine – his hair stayed flat. "I told you the speaker is a *male isoga*. You remember? Please notice that his hair is covered?"

Drey *had* noticed. In fact, it was the first thing he'd noticed about the vid. Tristol *never* covered his hair. From what he could tell, the tubular strands were sensitive as well as reactive. He wondered if it even felt pleasant, to have fabric confining a galoi's hair?

"When Drey and I go aboard to investigate, some galoi he encounters will be veiled."

"Is it religious?" Professor Frills's voice was sweet and soft – too nice. "It has been noted among academics that the galoi occasionally veil their hair. But it doesn't appear to be gender-associated, nor any particular form of trade or rank. We have been mystified by the veil."

Tris glanced at him and then back at Drey.

"It denotes a lack of trust, doesn't it?" said Drey. After all, he was a detective.

Tristol smiled at him, still tense and worried, but this smile was genuine – a few strands of his lavender hair lifted in pleasure at Drey's acuity. Drey basked in the approval. Amazed at himself, responding so profoundly to the shifting of a few purple locks. *Lavender locks. Lavender. Fuck, I am so very gone on this man.*

"Exactly. Our hair is a major component of communication. Like humans' eyes or face wrinkles or other body language. To cover the hair is to deny others understanding. This will make your investigation more difficult, Detective Hastion. *Taking the veil* is a matter of choice and a statement of insult."

Drey nodded, unsurprised. "Would the guilty party be more likely to wear the veil, do you think? Or leave it off in a brazen attempt to display innocence?"

Tris clearly hadn't considered either. "Good question. I will have to think about that. Outright deception is not common among the galoi. Misdirection hides in truth and nuance. So a veil could mean either."

Tris relaxed back at that and the superiors took over the discussion.

Eventually they were allowed to leave the briefing. Tris helped to craft the reply vid-message, in galactic standard, not galoi. Tris explained that it would not do to give them the advantage of their own language. It would be fun to respond in galactic standard, he said, for the galoi would be challenged and confused by the innate casualness and imprecision of the language.

Ambassador Quinn recorded the reply, at Tristol's suggestion. He accepted the opening barter on behalf of the station's humans, and offered Drey's services. And he relayed a long list of trade goods the station required in exchange. They must ask for something. Tristol had insisted that they request a great deal, because it increased the value of Drey's expertise in the eyes of the galoi. It also made Drey nervous. There were now valuable assets riding on his solving a crime.

Drey turned to Tristol as they left the briefing. "I'll be very happy to have you with me on that ship."

Tris wore a funny expression, hard to interpret and his hair was – what? – neutral, maybe. "And I am happy to be going with you, of course, detective. Always." They were still surrounded by their respective superiors so Tris kept things formal. "But I wonder if this is a good idea. They are meant to not know me or see me. But they will, and I will have to be careful about what I say and do. There could be repercussions."

Drey thought he understood a little. "Because you don't exist to them, neither of you can control the interaction, and that's frightening to galoi."

Tris blinked at him with those amazing eyes. Drey hadn't realized that purple could have so much depth. "Yes, how did you know that?"

"Baby, you have a language that is built on precision and you come from a culture where place in society dominates all conversation, it seems logical to me."

Tris nodded. They were walking together now, separated from the rest, heading toward the hub.

"But Drey, I also do not want you defenseless among my people. So we will do this together."

They reached the transport hub and floated together to Zone 3.

Tris grabbed his courage with all strands once they were back in gravity. He was not sure if Drey was still interested. Now Drey knew exactly how far Tris had fallen in the eyes of the galoi. Now Drey also knew more about how very odd and pedantic his people were, by human standards of behavior. Perhaps now Drey thought Tristol Zyga would be too much work.

He remembered what so many of his previous lovers had done to tempt him into sex, and decided that if he must act a little *antiga* to get what he wanted, he would try. So he said, "Would you like to come back to my quarters, detective?"

"Have you eaten yet today, baby?" was Drey's response.

Tris decided that no matter how much he thought the term *baby* a little weird, he liked it coming out of Drey's mouth. Possibly more than he liked *honey*. *Baby* was said with such profound affection.

"No. Mister Montiguous was more important and then we had the briefing. Should we get ramen? It is very tasty. I like the noodles, and perhaps I should apologize for Mister Montiguous being so forthright with the stall."

"One should never apologize for a cat," advised Drey, touching his still-healing scratches, much to Tristol's confusion. What did that mean? "But yes, let's get noodles and then…"

Was he nervous too? Was that a good sign? Tris was hopeful. *Think like an* antiga, he reminded himself. "And then my place?"

"Yeah, I'd like that."

Tristol could not stop his hair from fluffing up and reaching for the big human in delight. Drey chuckled and slid smoothly closer as they walked through the hawker center, putting his body within range. Tristol's hair slid along the silkiness of Drey's forearms, where they peeked out from his shirt. One strand wrapped lovingly around the human's wrist. The universe was a wonderful place.

Mistress Zing was delighted to see them. And seemed even more delighted to see them *together*. Xer eyes focused on Tristol's hair where it coiled in vibrant color contrast around Drey's dark wrist. Once, Tris would have thought that ugly. Now it was almost beautiful.

"Boys! You came back."

"This time without the cat," said Drey.

"You want ramen then?"

"Yes please!" Tris couldn't stop himself from bouncing a bit. But the cooks never minded. It seemed that excitement about food was considered complimentary on this space station. And Tristol was happy to get excited.

"You eating it here?"

Tris exchanged a shy glance with Drey. "Is that acceptable?" Would it be all right for them to be seen in public eating together?

Drey nodded. "It's a date. I'm honored to be seen with you."

Tristol's hair, still petting the big human, coiled tighter about him in pleasure. As if he were a galoi himself and knew the best response, Drey lifted his other hand and softly stroked two fingers down the lavender locks winding around him. Tris shivered in pleasure.

"Let's eat fast though, okay?" Drey's voice had dropped slightly in arousal. Tris knew that reaction. He was thrilled by it. Some humans had been a little perturbed by what they called *his hair thing*. Drey seemed to be the opposite.

They took their noodles to the park area. An open spot full of vegetative matter, most of it food-producing in some way, but still attractive and comforting. Tris always liked how it smelled, not that scent was a strong sense for him, but the greenness of it was nice. There were mats, suspension seats, benches, and tables. Drey led them to a table and they tucked in.

Humans ate with something called chopsticks. Most of them carried a personal telescoping set about their body at all times. Tris rarely remembered his, but the cooks had learned to just lend him a spare set, which he returned after using. Chopsticks were one of the hardest things to learn to use when he first left Gal. The idea of eating with two long pieces of metal held between the fingers was strange enough, but actually using them also proved initially impossible. Now, however, he was passing good. Tris slurped his noodles and drank the broth from the bowl like a native human. At least he hoped he did. He did not want to embarrass himself in front of Drey *on a date*. A real proper human date.

"Please do not tell the others, but I think Mistress Zing is my favorite cook."

Drey nodded. "Me too."

"But I have never seen you there before."

Drey took a fortifying breath. "That's because I always saw you first, so I went somewhere else."

"You did? Oh." *Why would he do that? Why would he avoid me?* "Did I do something wrong?"

Drey finished a mouthful. "No, baby. That's the problem. I liked you a lot, from the start. But I thought you weren't interested in the kind of relationship I want, so I figured I'd stay away."

"Oh!" Tris brightened. "You were keeping yourself from being emotionally injured?"

Drey nodded.

Tris was amazed that the human thought so well of him that he, Tris, had the power to affect Drey's actions. Still, he needed to be certain. "Because you thought I did not want to stay with you?"

"Exactly. We should make sure to talk about this kind of thing from here on out, okay? I don't always understand you, even with the hair."

Tris couldn't help but trill a bit at the request, inadvertent and relatively soft. Communication asked for was the nicest thing one creature could do for another. The need to understand was a joy and a gift. "I will try to tell you anything you need to know." He made it a vow.

"So in that spirit, the noise you just made. It's like a purr from a cat?" Drey grimaced as if he offered insult with the question.

Tris was not at all offended by the comparison. He thought very highly of cats. "A little. It is an expression of pleasure."

Drey's voice lowered. "Will you make it when we are in bed together?" His eyes had turned very dark.

Tris could hardly stop himself from making the trill again, right then and there, just because of the human's hungry expression. "I suspect, with you, I may make it a whole lot."

Drey grinned. "I look forward to the challenge."

Tris considered their now-empty bowls. "Should we go now, or should the date continue in a public venue with some walking around together?"

Drey shifted in apparent discomfort, but his eyes were still hot and dark on Tris. "Oh, I think we should go to your place now."

They cleaned their table and returned the bowls (and Tristol's chopsticks) to Mistress Zing.

"You boys be good now."

"I certainly hope not," responded Drey, which made the cook laugh.

It occurred to Tris to be a little nervous. "I should warn you, Drey, that my quarters are not like yours."

"That'd be nice, mine are depressing."

"Oh, not like that, I mean I do not have them arranged the way humans do."

"Good, I want to see what it's like. I need to know for the future anyway."

"You will never be allowed in a galoi's private quarters on the spaceship."

"I'll have to see the victim's room at least, Tris."

Tris flinched. "Oh yes, of course. I suppose it is possible that is where he died."

"Was killed."

Tris corrected himself with the alien concept. "Was killed." He brightened. "In that case, this will be a kind of preparation for you. Although, of course, I have had to adapt my style to your human arrangement of rooms. Here we are." They arrived back at his quarters and Tris unsealed the door with a flourish.

# THE 6<sup>TH</sup> CHAPTER

## *Coordinating colors and other intimacies*

The lights were dim in Tristol's quarters, but Drey could still see that the living room was set up very strangely.

Tris had warned him. The pretty man was already learning how best to communicate with Drey. He wondered if it was galoi nature to adapt to a partner's needs, but that seemed so unlike the rigidity he'd seen on that vid screen. Perhaps it was just Tris, or perhaps it was something to do with *loga.*

Drey was nervous about that. He didn't really understand the five-gender thing and he was worried, going in, that he might hurt Tris physically, if he didn't comprehend fully. But Tris had said he had a cock and he wanted penetration so Drey hoped that the mechanics were similar.

But the man's quarters were, well, odd.

The entire floor of Tristol's living room was covered in mattresses and blankets with pillows piled everywhere. There was no other furniture – no tables, no chairs, no couches. It was, basically, one massive bed. Drey did feel awfully tempted, in an entirely childish manner, to dive onto it.

There were no shelves, and no decorative items of any kind, no art hung on display. Instead, Tris had painted the walls, like an abstract mural. He'd used bold brushstrokes and cohesive colors, warm mauves and pinks darkening upward into muted violet, like a sunset. The ceiling was also painted, a dark warm gray-purple – like the night sky before the stars come out. Tristol's many pillows and blankets all went along with the color palette. It was comforting and lovely and a bit breathtaking and, Drey realized with no little amusement, perfectly matched Tristol's own lavender coloring.

"It's beautiful," said Drey, meaning it.

Tristol's hair fluffed in pleasure at the compliment. Such a simple thing to make this lovely man so very happy. "Thank you. It is *loga* nature to nest, to make a home. I had only my own colors to work with, though." He looked at Drey thoughtfully. "I should like to see you naked there, to know, but I think you will be perfectly coordinated."

Drey flushed at the brashness of that statement, but was also thrilled by it.

Then Tris broke his heart a little with his next idea. "Your skin is so beautiful, Drey. Perhaps I will get to add a little dark brown to it someday. If I am very lucky."

Drey had never had a man talk like he belonged to him before. Like he should change an environment to match him, to comfort. "Aesthetics are important to galoi?" he said at last, because anything else would be sappy. They hadn't even slept together yet.

"You should feel safe here," replied Tris, firmly, not answering the question. Or maybe that was the answer.

Drey wondered, Tristol's eyes being that much bigger than a human's, if he saw more nuances of color. Then he wondered if Tris was sensitive to the bright light of the day shift hallways, and if that was why he tended to work swing shift and keep his quarters dim. "Your eyes are more light-sensitive than ours, aren't they?"

Tris nodded. "And my ears are more sensitive too, particularly to lower vibration ranges. But our sense of smell is not so good. You will have to tell me if I offend in that direction."

Drey smiled. "And you'll have to tell me if I wear something that offends." His standard uniform on-duty was a dark gray, and his preference off-duty was for an old-fashioned black t-shirt and jeans. He knew his taste was plain, but he didn't really care.

Tristol's eyes shone. "You would let me *dress* you, as if I were your *somate*? Oh, you are kind."

Drey realized he'd accidentally given Tris a gift. This wouldn't be easy, dating an alien. And yet what he offered so casually seemed to please Tris so greatly, he supposed that it was going well so far. Drey really didn't care much how he looked. If Tris wanted to take that on, picking his outfits and shopping for them in the future, Drey would be more than fine with it.

He wondered what he might offer in exchange. He drew his eyes forcibly away from the beautiful living room that was no living room, but Tristol's *nest*, and turned to the kitchen.

All personal quarters on a space station were small – they had to be, with tiny galley kitchens and connected dining-meets-living rooms. All had short hallways with one bathroom and one bedroom. For larger families there were units with an additional bedroom. More than four as a familial unit was not considered space- or oxygen-efficient by station specs. Large families must remain planet-side.

There was nothing in Tristol's kitchen but a bunch of plants which were, apparently, what he used the sink for. Plants hung from the ceiling like chandeliers. Drey smiled to see it.

"In exchange for doing the shopping, how about I take over cooking duties?"

Tristol eyes were shining again, big and purple and so happy. "You would *cook*? For me?"

Suddenly Drey had an armful of lavender alien. Tris smelled amazing, treeflower-scented, like the almond

blossoms his sister still grew on his home planet. Drey
wondered if Tris even knew that about himself.

"Tris, I may have to ask questions as we do this. It's my
first time with a galoi."

"You may ask me anything." Tris breathed into his
neck, cool and comforting. "And I want to please you, so I
may ask questions as well. Like this, may I do this?" Soft
lips were against Drey's neck, pressing tiny kisses on his
throat. Then Tris began nuzzling against Drey's beard.

"You like my scruff?"

"Scruff?"

"My facial hair."

"Oh yes. It is a little rough. It makes my skin tingle."
Tristol's hair began to caress Drey's beard too, but then
quickly moved down to Drey's neck.

Drey chuckled. "Perhaps too rough for your hair?

"Yes, the strands are sensitive. I should like to wrap
them around your penis. May I do that sometime, Drey?"

Drey gasped and the organ in question throbbed. "Yes,"
he growled. "Please." He'd no idea he would like that
possibility so very much, but he really did.

Tris trilled in pleasure at Drey's enthusiastic response
and continued nuzzling Drey's face and caressing his neck.

They were still standing and they were still fully
clothed. Drey thought both these things totally absurd but
he didn't want to move and break the spell.

Tris whimpered and undulated against him. Somehow
both Drey's arms were now wrapped around the man's
slender form and Tris was plastered up against every part
of his body.

"You are so warm, Drey. Honey. Baby. No, I will find
something else. Softness? Mmm. Scruffiness?" Tris
bunted into him again, nose pressed to his neck, still
kissing.

Now Drey had incontrovertible proof that Tris was
male. He could feel the galoi's cock nudging his leg. Drey

swiveled his hips and bent his knees so their groins were pressed together, separated only by clothing.

"I should get naked," said Tris on a sigh. "I am making a mess of my nice pants."

Drey figured they'd established a need to communicate, so he asked, "You leak a lot?" His own voice was low and slurred with arousal.

Tris tilted his head back and gave him a coy smile. "Just you wait, Drey, you will like that part a lot, I think. My other human lovers have been pleasantly surprised by this aspect of *male loga* anatomy."

Drey wasn't totally happy to have Tris bring up other lovers at this precise moment but he was also fascinated by the fact that for the first time in their acquaintance Tris had specified a gender alongside the word *loga*. "What are the five genders, then, Tris?"

Tris was still dreamy and writhing in his arms so Drey took the initiative and began to steer them toward the mattress-covered living room. He wondered idly what Tris had done with his actual bedroom, but decided that could wait.

They folded down together into the welcoming cushioned softness. It was like falling into a sunset-colored cloud.

"Well, there is *antiga*, like you. Males who can get someone pregnant. *Isoga,* what humans might call neuter, although it is not exactly correct. They come in two variants, *female* or *male*. And us, *loga*, we also come in *female* and *male* variants."

Drey nodded, not fully understanding but pleased to have it all laid out at last. "Can we get naked now?"

Tristol wriggled about in his nest trying to get out of his suit jacket and shirt. But he refused to stop touching Drey and his hair kept getting caught on sleeves and collars, so it took longer than it should. This only made Tristol more frantic. Drey hid a smile. Then the little alien squirmed out of his trousers, or started to, only to discover that he still had shoes on. In a flurry of annoyance Tris tossed shoes and socks and then, finally, pants indiscriminately at the door. Which was closed and sealed, thank heavens.

Drey had meant to strip himself as well but he couldn't tear his eyes away from the galoi's writhing form. So he lay back, watching Tristol's enthusiastic antics. Drey's mouth watered. He must look like an enchanted idiot, as Tris revealed one lavender part of himself after another.

The galoi's skin was hairless. His body was lean with modest muscle definition, but nothing outrageously alien. Tristol was, in fact, Drey's ideal body type. Or would have been, if Drey had known to imagine lavender skin. Drey preferred men who didn't look like him – he adored the contrast of slenderness against his own bulk.

Tris couldn't be more perfect.

There were differences, of course. He was an alien. Drey scrambled to his knees and crawled forward to touch at last. He was still fully clothed while Tris was now lying naked in a field of sunset pillows, but it was perfect.

"You haven't any nipples," he said, reaching up to smooth his big hands over Tristol's pecs.

"No. I do not feed the young," said Tris.

"Neither do human males, but we still have nipples."

"Oh, really?" Tris was genuinely confused. "I thought that was part of the family grouping to care for young. I thought females did the birthing and males did the feeding, and that was why you had nipples."

Drey tried not to laugh. "No, baby, it's a vestigial sex characteristic."

"They serve no purpose at all?"

Drey gave a small smile. "Well, mine are pretty sensitive. So that's nice."

Tristol's eyes brightened. "Are they really? May I touch?"

Drey leaned back on his heels and whipped off his t-shirt, throwing it toward Tristol's pile of clothing. "Please."

"Oh, and you have hair on your chest too. I love it when humans do that." Tristol bent forward and his fine slender fingers brushed over the coarse, coiled hair on Drey's chest, a sensation Drey loved. Then Tris found his nipples.

The galoi was cautious with him at first, tentative with the little nubs.

"You can be rougher, pinch a bit."

Tris did. "Oh, I like that noise you made." And he did it again.

Drey lost himself to the sharp thrill, taking a while to notice that Tristol's hair was caressing his back, smoothing down around his shoulder blades, as far as the strands could reach.

"Are you consciously able to control your hair?" he asked, and then gasped when Tris tweaked his nipples again.

They'd somehow switched positions so Drey was lying back and Tris leaning over to touch Drey's chest. Drey lifted his hands to cup that perfect round lavender ass and pull him closer.

Tristol clearly wanted to collapse down onto Drey, but Drey stopped him. "Wait, I want to explore more."

Tris took a shaky breath and straightened up, sitting back on his heels. Drey sat up as well, began running his fingertips lightly over every part of that amazing svelte body.

Tris was hairless everywhere, including the groin area. His cock was gorgeous, pretty as he was, and flushed a slightly darker purple. *Not lavender there*. It clearly became engorged like a human's but Tris had no foreskin. Also he was leaking a lot more than a human did. He didn't have balls or a sack – instead there was a ring all the way around the base. When Drey touched it gently, it pulsed and another large drop of pre-cum oozed from the tip of Tristol's cock.

Drey thought it was utterly beautiful. He caressed again. Tris shuddered and more pre-cum emerged. Drey drew his hand up Tristol's cock, gently, not sure on grip strength.

Tris trilled in pleasure.

His pre-cum was amazingly smooth and slick, like the very best kind of lube.

Drey understood Tristol's earlier comment and chuckled. He pulled his hand back, testing the substance between his fingers. "This is what you meant, wasn't it? About a pleasant surprise?"

Without waiting for an answer, he reached forward and stroked again, and again Tris trilled and produced more pre-cum.

"Your pre-cum is essentially the best lube ever."

Tris moaned and jerked a little. "Of course it is. The purpose is to facilitate penetration." He gasped. "Remember what I said?"

"In order to climax you need to be fucked. Yeah baby, I remember. And this stuff would make fucking you wonderfully slick and fun, now wouldn't it?" He jacked Tris again, slow and easy, just to watch more liquid seep out the tip.

Tristol writhed for him, collapsing forward and against him, his hair wiggling like crazy. He forgot to play with Drey's nipples and was mostly passive – except his hair, of course – while Drey stroked and toyed with him.

Drey was unbelievably delighted with the whole experience.

"It is not *pre*-cum. It is…" Tris lost his explanation to another shuddering trill as Drey slid his big hand up and down again.

Drey flushed and his own neglected cock, trapped in his pants and throbbing with need, jerked at the implication of these words. "Are these tiny orgasms, baby?"

Tris whined and convulsed when Drey stopped jacking him, just cupped his big hand about the swollen ring of flesh at the base.

"Yesss," hissed Tris, hair frantic. He pushed against Drey's unmoving grip, trying to get Drey's hand to stroke again.

"But you can't entirely climax this way, can you?"

"No, but it is good. Very good."

Drey stood abruptly, suddenly desperate to get naked himself.

Tristol's eyes blinked opened and he smiled up at him, a slow display of sharp teeth.

Drey wondered what those teeth would feel like on him and then remembered what Tris had implied about preferences and *antiga,* so decided just to ask.

"Would you nibble on me a bit, Tris? Don't break skin. It's just for the sensation."

Tris trilled again, either overcome with the idea or from being asked to perform a service, it was hard to know which. Then Drey was distracted from removing his pants because Tris surged to his feet and was all over him. He remembered what Drey had said about his nipples and he'd been paying close attention to Drey's reaction when he nuzzled his neck. He started by nipping him lightly all over the throat and upper chest working his way down to Drey's nipples and then back up again.

Drey's skin tingled at the sharp pinpricks from pointed teeth. It was an amazing sensation. He'd always liked being bitten but humans had such blunt square teeth. Tristol's were sharper. Drey almost forgot he was taking his pants off.

*Almost.*

Finally, he was naked.

Tris shifted against him, leaned back a moment and suddenly everything stopped.

Drey blinked his eyes open.

Tristol was staring down at Drey's cock in either horror or amazement. "Drey, when you get very aroused your penis turns purple! For me?"

"Comes with the heritage, baby. You like?"

"Purple, Drey!"

"But not lavender, I'm afraid."

"No, it is a dark violet shade. It is *beautiful*. I didn't know humans could be purple."

"Only that part."

"Purple forever," trilled Tris.

"Christ, I certainly hope not. That brings new shades to the term blue balls."

Then Tris was back pressed against him, teeth clamping about his trapezius muscle, one slender leg wrapped around Drey's thigh, the other on toe-tips, rubbing his lube-slick cock against Drey.

Drey's knees gave out and he fell backward, Tris plastered atop him. They landed back in the soft cloud of Tristol's nest. Tristol's lean lavender body gloriously sprawled over Drey.

Tris was trilling again, but his movements were increasingly frenzied now. His hips swiveled desperately, and his trills were almost keens of want. He'd produced a lot of that amazing almost-cum slick. It oiled their bellies and made Drey so hungry for the man's ass his vision was clouding.

Suddenly Tris shifted back, leaning up on Drey's chest. His eyes were a deep midnight purple.

"Drey," he forced out words instead of trills but the music was there, in them, drawing out the consonants, fluttering vowels. "I need you inside. I need—"

Drey thought that sometime it would be fun to draw this out. To push that sinuous lavender body until Tris had no words at all. Until he forgot everything. But not this first time. Because fuck, Tris was right – Drey needed to be inside him like nothing else.

But Drey was also on the larger end of the spectrum and he'd never taken a man without a lot of preparation. Charmed by the fact that he could reach for Tristol's cock instead of the lube, he stroked up and gathered a pulse of slick from his lover's slit, then reached down and around, inserting one finger very gently.

Tris trilled and pulsed and gyrated on top of him.

"Okay baby, I'll give it to you, I promise. Calm down."

But Tris seemed almost manic now. Lost. He sat back hard on Drey's finger, grabbed at his own cock, not in order to get himself off, but in order to gather more slick. Then he reached behind himself and began to coat Drey's cock, eyes glazed in concentration. His touch was very light and gentle, which Drey supposed was an indication that he should keep his own that way. He'd have to tell Tris that he needed a firmer grip to climax. Tris harvested more lube from his own cock and then stroked Drey again, face blissful, learning the size and weight of Drey. Clever fingers dipped to explore his balls, which Drey supposed Tris probably found unusual and intriguing. Or he hoped he did – Drey loved to have them played with. But Tristol's focus quickly returned to Drey's cock and trying to get it inside him as soon as possible.

Drey was not about to deny him. He'd have to be insane to do that. But he did urge caution.

"Wait, baby, I'm really big. We need to stretch—"

But Tris was beyond that. Too impatient to hear reason.

Tris arched up, yanked himself off Drey's finger, and batted his hands away. He shifted back, finding Drey's cock, and impaled himself in one swift, sure movement.

That would have broken most human men. Even with Drey's one long-term boyfriend, they'd needed a great deal of prep work every time. Drey just had to hope that Tristol's alien biology made him different. He watched the galoi's face closely. There was absolutely no pain there, just pure bliss. Tristol's purple eyes were closed, his head was thrown back but he sank unflinchingly down. It was, without question, the most beautiful thing Drey had ever seen in his entire life.

Drey brought his hands to the man's lavender hips to keep him still, to force him to at least acclimatize to Drey's girth and length. Tris was already writhing on him. But he could do nothing more than undulate as Drey held him firm, a lot stronger than he was.

Tris opened his eyes and glared.

"I need to move, please, Drey?"

For the first time he noticed Drey's concerned expression. As if now that Drey's cock was exactly where Tris wanted it to be, he remembered that cock was attached to a person, and that person was worried about him.

The lavender returned to his eyes. His features, taut with need, relaxed a little.

"Drey," he murmured, and then bent over to nuzzle Drey's chest hair. "Drey, I am well." He shifted forward, off Drey's cock, to press his cheek to Drey's beard. "Drey, *loga* are made for this. You are a little longer than most *antiga* but that is good." He sank back, showing Drey how much he enjoyed it. "Since you have no barb, you will hit me just right inside. Please move, *somate*, please."

Drey suspected Tris had found him a pet name. *Somate.* He liked it. He also figured the man knew his own body, certainly better than Drey did, so he relaxed his grip.

Tris lifted himself up with a small moan and then dropped down onto him hard with a trill of bliss. Drey watched as his full length disappeared into Tristol's willing body. Tristol's own cock pulsed and released as he bottomed out – clearly there was something like a prostate deep inside him that Drey's cock hit and caused him profound pleasure. He suspected that was what Tris meant when he said he *required* penetration.

"What do you need, baby? Deep is good but do you want long and slow or fast and hard?" God, he wanted to take him. He wanted to flip Tris over and pound into him and forget everything. He'd never done that. Never felt with a human lover that he could be so forceful. They were too easy to damage with his stupid-big dong.

But Tris seemed to be sinking down ever harder each time. Driving himself onto Drey with such force Drey would have winced, had Tris been human. But he clearly wasn't in any pain at all. Drey was going to have to trust this. Trust him.

Tris opened his eyes once more. They were dark purple again. "I need it as hard as you can go, oh please."

So Drey did as his lover required, and as Drey wanted, and flipped Tris to lie on his back, and drove into him.

Tris wound strong lavender legs around Drey's hips and Drey pistoned, deep and fast, searching Tristol's face and his cock for the right reaction, until Drey knew exactly the correct angle (different location than the prostate, definitely deeper and more toward the tailbone) and let himself go completely. He fucked Tris hard as he wanted, watching with spine-tingling rapture as Tristol came totally apart beneath him. Losing all his words to moaning trills and eventually a melodic purring wail. Drey's stomach became coated in the most slippery cum ever, and he realized, surprised, that he too was climaxing, pulsing deep inside this perfect man.

He didn't collapse onto Tris. Drey was ever aware of his size with his lovers, in all ways, but he did want to stay connected. So he cradled around the limp purple body, and lifted and twisted so that Tris was sprawled on top of him once again.

Tristol's hair formed a lazy undulating luminescence around them. It was restful and calming like kelp under the ocean. Although Tris himself was utterly boneless and satiated, his hair still managed a gentle dance, caressing whatever parts of Drey it could reach, lovingly.

Drey had to check. "Okay, baby?"

Tris gave a slow slurred trill of sleepy happiness.

"Can I touch your hair?"

Another little trill, which Drey took as permission. He

was learning much about his lover's pleasure already and gloried in it.

Gently, very gently, he smoothed one hand down the waving strands. Tris melted against Drey even more, if possible. So Drey kept petting, marveling at the silken softness.

The trills resolved themselves eventually into galoi words, and from there into galactic standard. "So good," Tris was saying, over and over and over, and mixed into that, "so mine, gonna stay, Drey, please, so good, so mine, gonna stay," and it was a litany of claiming that drove itself straight into Drey's heart, where it coiled and caressed like Tristol's hair.

*My heart is turning purple,* Drey thought. And with one hand still smoothing through fat tubular silken strands, he used the other to press Tristol closer, to keep him.

Tris hadn't actually thought it was possible. Not with a human, not like that. He'd had fun with his human lovers, and he'd climaxed once he learned how to ask for what he needed.

But Drey, so exactly right from his build to his textures to his big hand stroking through Tristol's hair. Drey did not know, and could not see, that Tris lacked the advocacy strand. He saw only that it was alive and beautiful. Tris had called Drey *somate* in the throes of ecstasy. Embarrassing and he hoped Drey hadn't heard – humans didn't do that, after all. Not right away.

Still Tris had thought he would never get to say that in his life. He had thought, in choosing to leave his people, he had left all options for that kind of union behind him. No *antiga* for this *loga*. No mating and no *mycota*, just lovers and never *somate*.

Tristol would have been fine to live his whole live that way. Because he had reconciled himself to giving up love along with everything else, when he left Gal. But here was Drey. Drey who wanted to date him, and fuck him, and maybe if he was very good, keep him. Drey was keeping him now, close and firm in his arms. Arms still scratched from a cat he had rescued for Tris.

Drey was not rolling away.

Drey was not sending Tris home, as all the others had.

Well, they were in Tristol's quarters so that would be difficult to do, but still: Drey was not leaving.

He was staying.

"Could it... Tris?" Drey's voice when it came was wrecked and hesitant. "Could it be just us, please baby?" Drey sounded hopeful and weak at the same time.

This was obviously a difficult thing to ask in human culture. Tristol hadn't known that. Or maybe Drey had asked before and stupid idiots who were not Tris had said *no*.

It was, however, an easy promise for a galoi to make. Especially one like Tris, who had only ever worn a single earring.

"Yes," Tris said, and felt the big body under him relax. "Just us, Drey." *Somate.* "You will date me and I will be so good and you will realize that we are matched." *And you will ask me to stay, or you will stay here with me. Where I will paint my walls with your colors and find pillows to complement your skin and your eyes and your hair. You will cook for us in this kitchen that has never been used, like a human husband does. And I will take such good care of you, you will never want to leave. And you will take such good care of me that I will forget this is not my home because you will become that for me.*

That was all too much, he figured, for a human when they had only just fucked once. Too soon. But Tris had a goal now, and he believed it was a good one. Worth striving for. So long as this stupid galoi ship did not mess it all up for him. If Drey did not go among Tristol's people and see something horrible by human standards. Tris was terrified of that. But also resigned. Because he may be separated from the galoi, but he was still galoi in his soul. Drey would have to know it all, eventually, if he were to truly stay and Tris could paint his walls and call him *somate* for real.

Tris sat up a little, amused by his own copious cum covering them both. It clung, glistening, to the hair on Drey's hard stomach and around Drey's now flaccid penis.

Drey was watching him watch them, brown eyes sleepy and heavy-lidded.

One big hand reached forward to touch the cord about Tristol's neck, curious about the earring that dangled from it.

"It's black," explained Tris. "And there is only one. I wonder, with you, with us being us, if I am justified in wearing it again." He smiled, heart fluttering at the idea. Perhaps they could find a stud for his left ear, some dark brown stone or metal, to represent Drey. Perhaps Drey would pierce it for him, as a true *somate* would, linking them together. He would mention it later. Much later. After Drey became accustomed to him. After he made himself indispensable and pretty and coordinated everything.

"I noticed that the *isoga* in the vid wore two earrings of different colors in one ear and two studs of the same in the other. But you don't."

"You noticed?"

"I notice everything about you. Instead, I find you have one around your neck and an empty hole in your ear. What's it mean, baby?"

Tris thought Drey would need to know this for his future as a detective aboard a galoi ship, so he might as well prepare him.

"The rings indicated sexual orientation. Each ring represents a different gender. So an *antiga* can wear up to four earrings, every color except black. Because black would be another *antiga* and that is taboo. But he may have sex with both *male* and *female isoga* and *loga*. *Loga* may wear up to three, being given the option of *antiga* and both *isoga*."

"But you have only one." Drey fingered the black ring where it nestled against Tristol's throat.

"I should not even wear it at all. To be *zyga* is to be without gender and that means no earrings and no sexual preference may be stated. Our slang term for both *zyga* and infants is *naked ears*."

Drey frowned. "Galoi children have no gender?"

Tris nodded. "It was a strange thing for me to learn about your species." And it had been – very strange. He still found it odd and was grateful he had no human friends with younglings, because this way he did not have to interface with them. "Galoi are born hermaphroditic, or that is the closest galactic standard word for it. Your species develops secondary sexual characteristics at puberty. My species develops *all* sexual characteristics at puberty."

Drey looked amazed. "Wow. That's kind of incredible."

"After acquiring biological sex, completing the maturation process, and acclimatizing to a gender state, we are given sexual teachers, from the other acceptable genders. I had coitus with *antiga*, *male isoga,* and *female isoga*. Then I chose my earrings. In my case, just the one, *antiga*. I have only ever been attracted to the black ring."

"So the man in the vid?"

Tris smiled – this was like teaching a youngling. "He wore a white ring and a black one. So his preferences are for *male loga* like me, and…" he let himself trail off. Drey was still playing with the black ring about Tristol's neck.

"And *antiga*," the detective finished for him, responding to the coaxing tone. "Tris, baby, are you missing something because I'm not *antiga*?"

Tris shook his head violently. "Absolutely not. You are perfect for me. The sexual organ that you lack is not one that I want." Drey's penis did not have an *antiga's* barb at the head. A pleasurable feature, of course, designed to pulse and hook into the seal of Tristol's womb. But as wonderful as it felt, Tris did not want to get pregnant. He never had. That was the whole problem. That was the cause of everything.

Drey nodded, not convinced. "*Antiga* have another organ?"

Tris shrugged. "Another part on the penis. It is a sperm sack that inflates at the tip, like a barb. It pulses to release sperm and is designed to facilitate pregnancy and cause *loga* climax. It is very nice-feeling, but considering what you just did to me, not at all necessary."

He thought he should make this abundantly clear. Humans had fragile egos and Drey had not been lacking in *any* way. "No *antiga* has ever made me feel as you did." Because with *antiga* there had always been fear of pregnancy, but with Drey he could be utterly relaxed and free.

Drey was smiling now. "That is why you like being pounded so hard?"

"Yesss," trilled Tris, remembering how wonderful it felt. "And why I am so happy your penis is lovely and big. The length and fullness is good." He shivered, becoming aroused again just thinking about it.

Drey rumbled in human amusement. His hand moved from the ring at Tristol's neck to the ring at the base of his penis, which seemed to fascinate him. "You ready to go again so soon?"

Tris could feel the trill beginning in his throat. Drey's hand was so large and warm and it felt very exciting. "Yes, but I know humans have a longer refractory period. So do *antiga* and *male isoga*. My capacity to recharge is quick." He gestured to his own hard penis which, when Drey squeezed gently, began producing cum again. The tiny orgasm shivered through Tris at the tightened grip. He released the trill he had been holding in.

"I love your noises," rumbled Drey.

"I am more like a female human in the matter of climax. Or so I have been told."

Drey grinned. "Multiple orgasms?"

Tris nodded and moaned as Drey began to tease him with long strokes. Gentle, thank heavens. One major difference between all galoi males – *antiga, isoga,* or *loga* – and humans was penis sensitivity. One could be almost *rough* with a human. A few of Tristol's human lovers had required a very firm grip. That had shocked him. Of course, Tristol's ass was delighted with this fact, as it meant Drey could pound into him without the possibility of self-harm. Or so Tris hoped.

"I need to be penetrated to come, though, remember."

Drey kept stroking him. "I will never forget that now, baby. But I would like to just tease you. Can I play with your body for a while until I'm ready to fuck you again?"

"Oh dear." Tristol was not certain he could take that. "Is that likely to take you a long time?"

"Oh yes." Drey's pleased rumble was back. He moved from under Tristol and arranged Tris so he was lying sprawled atop various pillows and Drey was looming over him with glittering merciless brown eyes.

"You aren't sore?" Drey asked, so thoughtful and careful with him.

"No, my penis is fine, but it might get sore if you play with it too long."

"Your cock is very sensitive, huh? But no, I was asking about your ass."

Tristol's hair shook in amusement. "No, lovely human, that part of me is unlikely to get sore. Your penis is not sore from thrusting into me so hard?"

It was Drey's turn to laugh. "Not even slightly,

although it could get there if we do it too much. But I'd love to find out where the pain point is."

"Oh, me too!" Tris decided to lie back and let Drey do as he wished. The big human was now running his hands over Tristol's legs in long smooth strokes.

Then Drey leaned forward to gently lick Tristol's penis. It wept appreciatively and Tris trilled in delight.

"Oh!" Drey breathed hot over Tristol's sensitive genitals in surprise. "You taste like burnt caramel."

"That is a good thing?"

"Oh yes. But I'm sorry to admit that mine will not taste so sweet."

Tris did not bother to correct him. He knew what human males tasted like and he enjoyed it very much. It reminded him of a shellfish delicacy from home that was highly prized and very expensive.

But he was happy to know that he tasted good to Drey. After all, only Drey's opinion really mattered. And Drey was obviously enjoying himself.

"Save some for later," said Tris.

Drey chuckled and licked him again – warm and smooth and wet and certain. *And mine.*

Tris felt worshiped and cared for. So he prepared to learn all about this new kind of human teasing, no matter how frustrating.

# THE 7<sup>TH</sup> CHAPTER

## *But we don't even have a word for it*

Drey supposed it was a good sign that the galoi ship wanted to move quickly. It was always better not to let a crime scene get cold. Yet he was reluctant to leave Tristol's warm nest.

They'd fucked again, eventually, after he teased Tris mercilessly for over an hour – learning all his erogenous zones and all his flavors. The curve of Tristol's lower back, the full length of his hair, the edges of his ears, all turned out to be wonderfully sensitive.

Of course, he woke in the middle of the night hours to find Tristol paying him back.

The galoi was exploring him, applying teeth and nails, being rougher with him because he'd already learned that Drey liked a bit of sharpness with his pleasure.

Drey had ended up fucking Tris again, because he couldn't help wanting to see him come utterly apart, because a man who produced his own lube was a galactic wonder, because Tristol's lavender hair danced while Tris rode Drey's cock and trilled out his joy. Nothing had ever been more beautiful. Nothing.

Which meant that when they were summoned to go aboard the galoi ship, negotiations having finally concluded, they were fuck-drunk and sleep-deprived, and sore in absolutely the best possible way.

They cleansed together and then Drey had to go back to his quarters to change. It turned out Tristol used his bedroom for clothing storage. His pretty pastel suits hung in a row on a solitary rack in the corner. His shoes were lined up against the wall next to it. That was all. Drey thought they might turn that room into an office when he moved in and then was amazed with himself for even thinking it. Fuck-drunk, indeed.

So they separated briefly and Drey ran back to his own quarters, lonely barren-walled and entirely lacking in sunsets.

His earpiece chirruped at him, directing him to the designated dock where he was to meet an alien spaceship and find a murderer.

It was possible that Tris was more nervous than Drey, when they met up outside the docking bay. After all, Tristol was the only one who knew what they were actually in for.

Professor Frills, Adjudicator Jones, and Ambassador Quinn were there as well.

"We aren't coming inside, I promise," said the adjudicator, before Tris could even open his mouth to make certain they abided by the rules of the trade.

The galoi had negotiated in a hard clause for no recording devices. His people weren't idiots.

Still, Professor Frills was there with a list of instructions for Drey. "Pay attention to galoi interpersonal interactions and culture. I'll want to completely debrief you, as soon as you are back aboard station."

Drey glared at the human. "I'm not sure how useful I'll be. This isn't my training and I'm going there to look for clues in a murder, not to be your culture spy."

Tris was delighted to realize that his *somate* did not like Frills either.

They entered the docking bay together, Drey slightly in front, Tris shadowing him. He thought that would be the best positioning, as that way no galoi would walk into him.

Sometimes galoi took *zyga* a little too literally.

The spaceship was new and shiny and modern. Tris had been on a galoi spaceship only once, when it took him and dumped him on an alien world for the first time. When it set him free.

It was pretty – most things the galoi made were pretty. Sleek and silvered and curved, designed for atmosphere even though it lived in space. Galoi never saved money or time at the expense of appearance. Impression was everything. How a ship looked spoke to how important it was, where it fit in the social hierarchy of other ships. This one was highly ranked.

Tris had almost forgotten that jolt of certain identity bred out of perfect aesthetics. Too long he'd been living among humans, where they believed, or pretended to believe, that *practical* was morally superior to *pretty*.

"It's beautiful." Drey's dark eyes were wide in awe.

"How a thing looks reflects its importance in life."

"Oh, am I dressed well enough?"

Tris was pleased to hear Drey worry about such a thing. "You look very well, severe and alien, and dark and foreboding. The dark gray marries well to your skin tones and you will set yourself apart while not appearing too much in contrast. It was a good choice."

"I'm in uniform, baby. I hardly had a choice."

"I know, but I like to pretend you put a great deal of forethought into such things."

Drey paused to look Tris up and down. "You did, I take it?"

"Yes. Only some will even bother to see me. Most will note the naked ear and I will not exist for them. But still, I am making a statement by wearing black. Galoi never wear black. It clashes. I am being intentionally ugly." Tris felt a little stiffness in his hair over his choice, but he needed them to know. His suit said many things to any galoi who cared to look. *I do not care. Your opinion no longer matters. I have embraced a new life. I am ugly and I am nothing but I am free.*

Tris was wearing one of his standard adorable close-cut suits, only it was black. Drey had never seen the man in anything but pastels before. He hadn't thought Tris liked dark colors.

Tris looked *amazing* in black. His lavender skin glowed against the velvet fabric. Also, Drey couldn't deny hundreds of years of conditioning that caused him to see black as formal, elegant, and dignified.

"You look gorgeous," he told his lover. Awed.

"I do? Oh, you actually mean that! I forget, humans admire contrast." His hair, which had been still and flat (with nerves, Drey suspected) puffed up a little at the compliment.

The gangplank to the galoi ship was down. Drey wondered if the galoi crew had explored the empty docking bay at all. How weird did the human space station seem to them? Or did galoi restrict their people's access to alien environments, as much as they restricted human access to them?

Drey took a breath and stepped onto the ramp.

Tristol was reassuringly close behind him.

The air emanating out of the open hatch was odd-smelling, almost earthy or mossy.

They topped the ramp and rounded the corner. There, hidden from any eyes or cameras below, stood a galoi Drey assumed must be the captain. The ship's hallway arched up and curved around so the man was only just visible, above and away from them. A power play, that they must keep walking toward him, looking up as if he were some ancient priestly king.

The man looked taller than Tris, but not by much, and had the same slenderness of frame and light musculature. He was severe and angular, without Tristol's appealing softness or cheerful demeanor. His skin was darker, too, still purple, but a deep violet color. He wore a navy robe, short, over matched wide-legged trousers. It complemented his skin tone and Drey realized he was already trained to think a little like Tris, that he noticed such a thing.

Tris plastered up against his side as they walked, slowing them both down. The contact jolted Drey with desire, but seemed more a vehicle for Tris to rise on tippy-toes and whisper in Drey's ear.

The galoi stared at Drey as he approached, examining him carefully from head to toe as if searching for clues.

Tris spoke fast and low. "This is the captain, *antiga*. He has four rings so he favors all genders. The two studs in his right ear indicate that he has two spouses, bonded *somates*, silver for *female loga* and copper for *female isoga*. They will be with him on this spaceship. Galoi do not separate spousal groups. Since he is also the captain and allowed off planet, we can assume that both he and his *loga* have contributed *gamein*."

"Remind me what that means?" whispered Drey back. They were almost close enough for the captain to hear.

Never once did the *antiga* look at Tristol – his gaze registered only Drey.

"Obligatory progeny. Three young each, to increase the population. So he will be proud, arrogant, perhaps a bit self-righteous."

"His hair is uncovered."

"Yes, so watch it."

The captain's hair was almost exactly the same color as his skin. It was shorter than Tristol's and perfectly still. Controlled.

Drey and Tris stopped in front of him, not too close.

Obeying the distance required for inter-species negotiations by galactic law.

Silence reigned. Tris had warned Drey that he could not address the captain first.

A larger galoi appeared up the hallway and strode fast to stand next to the captain and a little in front of him. She had breasts so Drey went with female. She had to be at least half a head taller than the captain, and had way more muscle mass. She was nowhere near as big as Drey, but very physically fit. She had the balanced stance of readiness, and the sharp eyes of caution. Her clothing was tight to her body and no doubt stretchy, so she could move easily. This one was trained to fight. Drey knew power when it resided in muscle memory. She was also magenta-colored.

Still no one spoke so Drey tilted his ear toward Tris. "Who's his friend?"

Tris gave him the rundown fast and hurried and hissed. "*Galoi*isoga*female*somate-to-antiga*somate-to-loga female*. See how she has black and silver studs in one ear? Her spouses are a *female loga* and an *antiga*. That matches to the captain but does not necessarily link them. She could be his spouse or perhaps the first mate of this ship or head of its security. I will need to hear them converse in galoi to know the nuances of their relationship. There is a good chance they will not talk to each other in our presence, for that exact reason. She will not be introduced to you."

"Her earrings are the same as her ear studs."

"Yes."

"But not the captain's?"

"One does not always get to marry *all* of one's sexual preferences."

Drey considered his various bisexual and pansexual friends and the relationships they'd settled into. He supposed that was true in humans too.

Although this conversation took place directly in front

of them, and both galoi could no doubt hear and understand, they did not acknowledge it.

Drey looked the captain over, giving him the same insulting perusal. This galoi was no fighter, and he seemed calm enough for a man with a murderer aboard.

Their eyes met. The *antiga's* were a vibrant eggplant color. Finally, he spoke. "You are Detective Hastion?" His galactic standard was extremely good. Almost as good as Tristol's.

"I am."

"I did not know humans came in such a pretty color profile."

"You must not have met many of us. I didn't know galoi came in such a dark purple."

"I am *antiga*."

Tristol whispered, "Darker pigmentation is considered a particularly attractive trait in the first gender."

The galoi captain made no further comment. His eyes continued to *not see* Tris. The guard's, however, did. They rested on the lavender man lightly and dismissively, but intently. She was evaluating all threats, even the ones that supposedly didn't exist.

The captain seemed to recollect himself. "Anisoi Ureeya. I will show you to your work."

No niceties here. No polite greeting needed.

The hallway was empty as Drey followed the captain and his *isoga* guard toward what he assumed was the crime scene.

Tris stuck close but seemed to have nothing more to say. Drey would have to ask about whatever he found confusing. To Tristol everything around them was normal. For the moment, Drey decided to simply absorb the strangeness of the alien spaceship and stay silent.

It was remarkably beautiful. The outside of the ship had appeared almost like a coiled seashell. The inside was similarly iridescent and organic. The wall, and there was only one, on the outer side, was mirrored, but misty and soft, made of some silvery material. The ceiling above was all silver pipes with beautiful flowering purple vines coiled around them. The flowers were tubular and hung downward, a very pale lilac with spots and speckles of darker purples. They gave off no flowery perfume, but Drey could guess they were responsible for the general vegetative smell that permeated the ship. No doubt they were heavy oxygen producers. The inner side of the hallway had no wall but simply circled what Drey assumed was the massive central engine of the spaceship. This too was beautiful, gleaming and mechanical, and incorporating organic components. He was no engineer to understand any of it, but he had certainly never seen anything like it before – a gorgeous functional sculpture, meant to be in a museum but instead running a spaceship.

They walked in silence – *antiga, isoga,* Drey, and Tris – through the hallway which seemed to now be coiling downward. They eventually branched off into a much narrower hall, with all the expected walls, and barely big enough for two to walk abreast. Each side was lined with oval doors which Drey assumed meant they were in a residence warren. He wondered how many faces were pressed to the view-scopes in those doors, looking at him. Staring at the alien. The first human ever allowed on a galoi ship. That's assuming they had view-scopes.

There was a sound to the hallway here, a faint chiming, like glass beads in a wooden tube. A different plant grew around the ceiling pipes. This one was pale green with thousands of small white flowers in sprays that dangled in large globules above them. They moved in a slight breeze.

"What's that noise?" asked Drey.

Anisoi Ureeya didn't answer him.

Tris did. "The flowers above us are singing as they generate airflow. They are called *alysigoss,* which is something like *plant*breeze*sing*breathe*."

Drey nodded and decided it was time to stop being awed and get to work. "Captain Ureeya, what can you tell me about the victim?"

Tristol's cool breath was against his ear again, and his slim form pressed against his side. Drey wanted to stop and gather him into a hug. He wanted to ward off the strangeness of this alien place with his alien boyfriend, as if *that* made any sense.

"You must call him *Anisoi* Ureeya. The identifier honorific is more important than his job title."

"So *anisoi* is like *mister*?"

"More. It means *\*antiga\*bonded\*completed-gamein\*productive\** member of society. It is a placement in the order of life."

"As *zyga* is a displacement?"

Cool lips met Drey's neck at that, a kiss for his understanding. "Yes."

The captain stopped in front of one of the doors and turned to stare at Drey. He seemed suddenly to both see and not see Tristol. He also, apparently, felt no compunction about acknowledging that he heard Drey's side of the conversations.

"You will not use that word, human detective."

"*Zyga*? Very well, Anisoi. This is the crime scene?"

"That is your term for it." The captain waved his hand before the door and it telescoped open.

The room looked oddly familiar. A small chamber that was covered in a single mattress with pillows and blankets in color-cohesive piles. The walls were painted to match. The ceiling was not, as it was composed of more of the small white flowers, interspersed with twinkling lights, like stars. Instead of a sunset, this room reminded Drey of a misty dawn. The paint strokes were less bold than on Tristol's, more dotted and diaphanous.

"He nested beautifully," said Drey.

The captain's hair twitched in surprise. That Drey knew

how to compliment a *loga*, or that Drey used the word *nest*? Difficult to tell.

But he managed to smooth his hair back down quickly enough.

Drey wondered if Tristol's lack of control over his hair was a product of youth, or exile, or personality, or gender. He found himself oddly grateful for it. It was comforting to know his lover couldn't, or didn't wish to, hide his feelings. Even now a lavender strand was pressed to Drey's arm for reassurance. Drey reached without looking and petted it softly with two fingers. Tristol's stiff form relaxed slightly.

In the middle of the nest was a mauve-colored body, naked and crumpled, but perfectly matched to the room about him. His hair was not just limp but flat, the tubes collapsed into lifeless ribbons.

Drey sighed, feeling a profound sense of sadness, struck by the idea that once this young man's hair had been as vibrant as Tristol's.

Then he shook off his melancholy and got to work.

It made Tristol unhappy.

All of it.

The pretty nest, empty of other colors but those that matched the *loga* who'd crafted it. The painting style was tentative, diaphanous, and hesitant. This *loga* had been unloved and lonely. It reminded Tris of his own nest on Gal, before he understood what he really needed. Before he left.

The *loga* himself was on the pinker end of the spectrum, which Tris thought was not as nice as his own skin tone, but still pretty. He had a heart-shaped face with fine features and soft lips. He was curled on his side with his eyes closed and his mouth slack. He had vomited onto the blankets in an arched spray.

Tris looked away, embarrassed for the dead *loga*.

Drey moved across the nest without flinching and bent over, not touching, just looking closely at the limp body. His shoe brushed through some of the sick, and Tris shuddered, hoping the *isoga* did not notice such human clumsiness.

"He was poisoned."

"Yes," snapped Anisoi Ureeya.

Tris shuddered. It was hard to poison a galoi, not with the two stomachs, both of them resilient. There were abrasive chemicals that did it, of course, and a few particularly vicious plants on Gal, and maybe an insect or two. But not much.

"With what?" Drey asked.

"Our physician is looking into that."

"I will need to talk to them."

"That is not possible. You will only be talking to me."

Drey straightened and turned. "You want to know who killed this boy?"

The captain's hair briefly flattened: *distress*worry* fear*. He got control of it quickly, however, too quickly. Tris was not sure anyone should trust an *antiga* with that level of emotional control. He certainly did not.

Tris darted a glance to the *isoga*. Her hair was veiled and her face utterly impassive. She watched Drey as if the human was about to pounce on her *antiga*. She did not look at the mauve-colored body. She did not look at Tris. He thought she might be watching him, though, out of the corner of her evil magenta eyes.

Drey was looking fierce and looming. He had that line in his forehead, the one that in humans meant anger. His voice was hard. "You traded for my skills but you prevent me from using them? How does that make logical sense? I will need to speak to your doctor myself."

"You may talk to Belloi Rissib only through me."

Drey rolled his eyes and returned to examining the body. "Tris, I need you."

Tristol moved to him quickly and without conscious thought, avoiding the vomit. He would do anything for Drey if Drey needed him. Nothing was better than to be wanted.

He explained in a low voice, because he thought that was what Drey needed. "Belloi Rissib is the name of a *female isoga*. Anisoi Ureeya's tone indicates respect for her. He may or may not trust her with you. He is restricting access to his crew for the sake of xenophobia, not for malicious purposes. Although it is hard to tell exact nuances when using galactic standard. His hair is very controlled. He could be hiding something."

Drey nodded. "Thank you, baby, but it's the victim I need your help with. His earrings. See? One is black for *antiga*, but what does the gold one mean? Or is that a variant on copper?"

"*Male isoga.*"

"And he has no studs."

Tris pressed against Drey's back and shut his eyes. He could not look at the poor crumpled body. "He had no *somate*. And his preference in sexual partners was for males. That is common with *male loga*."

He could feel Drey's rumbling chuckle, although the human kept it from leaking out. "Your gender tends to be gay, huh?"

Tris bit him lightly through his shirt. "Stop limiting galoi with your puerile human definitions of sexual orientation."

"But I like that you're gay!"

"Behave, detective. Do you not have a crime scene to investigate?"

"Stop trying to climb me and get a piggyback ride out of it, then."

Tris pulled away instantly, hurt. *Pigs? Pork? Food behavior?*

Drey turned and noticed his wilt. "I was teasing, baby. I like that you want to touch and be close to me, just not while I'm working, okay? Or at least, not actually on top of me while I'm working? We have an audience. Well, I have an audience."

Tris nodded, his hair still flat.

Drey looked over at the other two galoi in the room.

They were looking at Drey but not at Tris, which must be difficult considering how close they stood to one another. Tris felt a bit self-satisfied about that. He was not making it easy for them to ignore him. He was also intent on staking a claim. *I may have no stud to prove it, but Drey is my* somate. *Mine.*

Drey sighed. "Come here, baby."

Tris notched up against that big warm body, fast and close.

Drey chuckled. "Okay, a compromise. How about you let your hair touch me for now as much as it needs. Will that suffice?"

Tris nodded and sighed in relief. Pulling away from the warmth was hard but letting a few strands of his hair rest against Drey's back as the human bent to look at the body was reassuring. This also allowed Tris to turn away slightly and watch the other two galoi in the room while Drey worked.

The galoi were clearly uncomfortable. But that was likely the result of having an alien near them. Or having a murder aboard their ship. Not, Tris suspected, because there was a *zyga* around.

They did not touch each other, but he got the impression of intimacy nevertheless. He was leaning more and more in favor of the *isoga* guard being one of Anisoi Ureeya's spouses.

Drey straightened and addressed Anisoi Ureeya. "What is the victim's name?"

"Ooloi Villisol."

Tris said to Drey. "Please ask him why a *loga* without *gamein* was aboard this ship."

Drey nodded. "Ooloi Villisol has not contributed children to grow your population?"

"He has not."

"Isn't that a requirement for space travel?"

"No. It is rare for a fertile *loga* to be allowed off planet without *gamein*, but Ooloi Villisol was an extraordinary engineer, so an exception was made in his case."

Tris perked up at that. Very interesting. "Drey, that means they have experimental technology aboard this ship." There was no doubt in his head, there was no other reason for an incomplete *loga* to be in space.

Anisoi Ureeya's gaze flicked to him briefly.

"Well, that is some kind of motive." Drey began to walk slowly about the nest, bending and examining the occasional pillow or blanket.

Everything was quiet for a long time.

Drey did not appear to find anything significant. He did one more pass close to the body, pulling Tris against him for a soft hug in an almost reverent manner, before leaving the nest to stand before the two galoi.

"Since he has no studs in his ears and there's no wailing spouse, I'm assuming he's not married."

"You assume correct."

"Any lovers?"

Anisoi Ureeya tilted his head, hair stiff. "Likely, yes."

"I'll need a list of names and I'll need to interview them."

"You will give me the questions and I will ask for you."

"No."

"There is no other way."

"I cannot find your murderer if you constantly stymie me. I need access to this *loga's* life in order to know how he died. And we can start with the doctor. When will you have the results of the poisoning?"

"It will take a while," Anisoi Ureeya hedged.

"Then I'll leave your ship now and take a break. And

during my absence you should think about whether you really want answers. Give me access to those I must interrogate and the information I need, let me do my job, or boost off my station and remain in ignorance with a murderer on your ship. You seem to enjoy being an idiot." He touched Tristol's arm. "Come on, baby, we're done here."

They moved to the door, which remained resolutely shut. Drey obviously wanted to storm out dramatically but didn't know how to operate a galoi seal.

Tris nipped in front of him, keeping his hair from shaking with amusement by pure will, and waved his hand through the appropriate air-space.

The door telescoped open.

"How did you do that?" Drey asked as they moved back down the warren hall.

Anisoi Ureeya and his *isoga* followed them, but Drey ignored them.

Tris was viscerally thrilled by the daring rudeness of it.

"How did I do what, detective?" Tris used the title even thought he wanted to pet the big human for his boldness and courage. Drey was so wonderfully alien, to *turn his back* on an *antiga*! To storm out. To demand contact. To demand *names*!

"Open the door?"

"Oh, there are sensor particles in the air at about this height. You use a motion like so." Tris demonstrated while they walked.

"But you don't exist, baby."

"The door does not know that."

"So you're still cleared to activate galoi gadgets from when you weren't in exile? They never stripped your clearance?"

They exited the warren and moved quickly up the main hallway. Tris took a moment to appreciate the *sillovin* blooms overhead. They were his favorite flower and he had missed them.

"Clearance, detective? What do you mean...? Oh! No. Anyone can open the door."

"To his *private* residence?" Drey was genuinely shocked.

"Of course. It is only a door."

Drey made a funny snort-moan noise. "This is going to be harder than I thought. You mean to tell me, the *entire ship* had access to that boy's quarters?"

"Yes. And *that boy* is likely older than you are."

Drey ignored the mild rebuke, still shocked by the door situation. Tris supposed humans did seem obsessed with locking and sealing things.

"That's a lot of suspects, Tris."

"Is it not exactly the same number we started with? All the ship's complement?"

"True." Drey chuckled.

Then they were out and back down the ramp into the echoing empty docking bay. Behind them the *antiga* and *isoga* stopped before they might be seen, wary.

"I need to talk over a few things with you, baby, but Frills is going to pounce the moment we open that door. Meet me later?"

Tris bounced only a little. "Another *date*?"

"Yeah, baby, but with some work in there. There's shit I don't understand and didn't know to ask you about before. Now I really need to ask. You have to help me out here, 'cause that goddam captain clearly doesn't want to make this easy."

"You want my help? I am honored. I will do my very best."

Drey smiled, brown eyes soft in that way Tris was beginning to realize was only for him.

"Okay, good. Hawker Zone 3 for lunch?"

"Noodles again?" Tris was hopeful.

"Noodles are fine, baby."

Tristol knew his hair was back to being overly fluffy.

Even after the sadness of that poor dead *loga*, he could not hide his pleasure in the fact that Drey had called him *baby* several times and wanted to eat noodles with him again.

# THE 8<sup>TH</sup> CHAPTER

*Socks, chopsticks, and second dates*

Drey was annoyed but that was, frankly, pretty normal on the first day of an investigation. He wasn't surprised the galoi had been uncooperative. He just had to hope he hadn't pushed them into leaving entirely. He wanted to catch the galoi who did it. *Fucking poison. Poor mauve-colored kid.*

He exited the docking bay under the eager gazes of the dignitaries collected there. He grabbed his com-pad and dictated a ton of notes, holding up a hand to keep anyone from interrupting him.

Adjudicator Jones was the only one brave enough to interrupt. "We'll leave you to your work, detective." She and Tris trundled off, much to Professor Frills' annoyance.

"You ought to leave your attaché, adjudicator!"

Tristol's boss was having none of it. "He has a job, professor, that does not include entertaining you."

Tris obediently followed her, hair quivering. Drey suspected that meant pride or joy at being protected by the adjudicator.

Ambassador Quinn settled back, leaning against the bulkhead, while Drey finished processing everything that had just happened. His own boss was accustomed to how he worked and wasn't even paying attention, muttering into her ear-com and pacing a little way away. He'd talk to her later, when he filed his official report.

Professor Frills twitched with ill-disguised impatience but Drey wanted to get all his thoughts and observations pertaining to the crime scene recorded as quickly as possible, while still fresh in his head. The anthropologist could wait.

When he was finished, he turned to the ambassador. "Situation unknown, sir. We're at an impasse. The captain is denying me access to his crew, even for investigative purposes, so I'm waiting him out. Either he really wants to know what happened, or the galoi ship will leave soon."

Frills squeaked at that.

Drey didn't look at him, instead turning to his boss. He waggled his fingers to get her attention. She disconnected from whoever she'd been on-com with and marched over.

"I've something for you."

She whipped out a specimen bag, prepared, and knowing Drey's quirks.

Drey sat down, right there on the hallway floor, and removed his right boot. "There's vomit on it from the victim. Full spectrum analysis, please. I want to know everything we can about this kid. Not just what killed him. What he ate, what he drank, anything we can get."

His boss bagged the shoe and grinned at him. "I take it the galoi have their own doctor on it already?"

"Yeah, but they won't let me talk to her."

"The more ammunition, the better. I'll get this in to Joel while you debrief with the professor."

Drey inclined his head. His boss grinned at him totally without sympathy. She knew he'd much rather talk to the lab-tech himself and that the last thing he wanted was to pause his investigation to argue points of culture with an academic.

"The galoi captain said they should have their results *in a while*, whatever that means. I think maybe the galoi get off on the imprecision of galactic standard, it's so different from their own language. So if we could get ours done in *less than a while,* that'd be great."

"You know as well as I do that the tests take as long as they take. And we're working blind, never had vomit from a galoi before. So we've no baseline for comparison."

Drey nodded and took off his other boot, because it would be plain stupid to walk around a space station with only one shoe on. He sent an affectionate *thank you* in Tristol's direction. His lover had said galoi were deceptive mainly in speech, which is how Drey knew he could get away with a deceptive *action*. Besides, who'd think to steal vomit? Tris certainly hadn't realized what Drey was doing. Even as Drey had used Tristol's body position to shield his feet from galoi view.

Drey returned his attention to the ambassador. "Anything else you need from me, sir?" *Oh please say yes.*

"Nope. I'm just gonna observe the professor in action."

"Here?" Drey was not excited about standing around in his socks in docking hall being interrogated by a pedantic intellectual.

"Come back to my office. We can at least sit there. I may even manage some tea." Frills tried to smile. It looked like it hurt.

Drey could use some tea, so he almost started to like the man.

An hour later, he actively hated him.

He'd had to describe *everything* in exacting detail. From the appearance of the spaceship interior, to the sound and smell in the hallways, to every nuanced gesture made by the captain and his *isoga* guard. He'd been asked to recite back the conversations they'd had. When Drey threw up his hands and explained that he didn't have a *fucking eidetic memory*, Frills ignored his outburst. Drey explained that he'd been observing interactions and unspoken behavior, and examining a very dead body. He didn't care as much for the words themselves, especially as they'd been speaking galactic standard. But Frills did. Oh boy, did he ever.

Drey intentionally kept much of what Tris had said a secret. Anything, in fact, that pertained to their relationship together was to be avoided. Drey didn't want some sleazy academic prying into his personal life.

Frills didn't seem to notice gaps. He was no detective, that's for certain. He merely recorded everything Drey said, also taking notes, and acting pompous about it.

Eventually Drey ended the interrogation himself, by standing up. His stomach was growling and he was worried about being late for his lunch date with Tris. "We're done here, professor."

"Oh, but I've so much more—"

"No. I've a lot to do before I'm called back aboard that ship. I've given you all I can."

"Oh but—"

Drey looked pointedly at the ambassador who'd been sitting in silent observation the entire time.

Ambassador Quinn was a solid negotiator. He understood. "Let the detective go, professor. Remember, his priority is fulfilling the terms of the trade, not satisfying your curiosity."

"But this is more than anyone has ever gotten on a galoi ship! That alone is worth more than any trade. This will materially advance our entire understanding of—"

"So go away and process it," barked Drey.

The ambassador was a much better diplomat. "I'm sure the detective will have plenty more for you next time."

"Oh he will, will he?" said Drey, vowing never to do this again.

The ambassador shook his head at Drey to silence him. "Off with you, detective, or you'll miss lunch."

Drey left as quickly as humanly possible, annoyed that it was too late to go to his quarters first and get shoes.

"Detective! You have no shoes on! Is that a ritual requirement of the second date among humans?" Tris bent over to take off his own polished loafers.

Drey, who was in only socks, gave him an amused look. "Yes indeed, being seen in public in only socks, together, is a declaration of romantic intent."

Tris could not take his shoes off fast enough. He was pleased he had chosen very pretty socks that day. They had a flowered motif that melded his own lavender skin tone with the black fabric of his suit.

"Of course you're wearing adorable socks." Drey sounded both grumpy and delighted.

Tristol wiggled his toes and wondered what to do with his loafers. Finally he just held them in one hand. He noticed Drey was holding one also. Was that also part of the second date ritual? Tris was awfully fond of shoes so he had memorized all the different names and types. Drey held a *boot*. Boot was a good word.

"What has happened to your other boot, Drey?"

"Gone for testing. Turns out I got a bit of the vomit from our victim on it."

"You did? How lucky!"

Drey gave him a very funny look.

"Oh, that was sarcasm! Drey, you did it on purpose? You stole poisoned vomit, to give to human scientists, so they could test it, and you could compare that to what Anisoi Ureeya tells you, and thus know if he is hiding something. You *are* a clever human." Tris went from accusatory to admiring during the course of one very long sentence. Humans could be so delightfully devious.

Which made Tris realize something else. "Being be-socked on a second date is not a real human ritual, is it?"

"No, baby."

"You were being sarcastic with me then too?"

"I was. But your socks really are cute."

"Thank you. I purchased them special when I realized I might have to wear a *black* suit some day." Tris was still not happy about the black – it clashed. But insults were sometimes necessary, and sometimes they were made with suits, especially among the galoi. The *isoga* had noticed and been offended. Of course, Tristol originally bought the suit with human bereavement rituals in mind, as well as formal galas and spousal contract parties. For some reason, all these desperate occasions demanded black.

"So, now that you realize I was kidding, you can put your shoes back on, baby."

Tris shrugged and sidled up to Drey so his hair could stroke over the big human's lovely hard bicep. "But then you would be the only one here, in a public forum, wearing socks."

Drey petted his hair with his free hand. "Ah, so you're insisting on sock solidarity?"

"I am."

"Or is it sock sympathy?"

"Well, yours are not very nice-looking. I should take you shopping."

"Yeah?"

"You would like that, me looking after you?"

"I already said I can't be bothered with how I dress. If you want to be bothered, I'd actually really appreciate it."

Tris nodded to himself. This was *wonderful*. Drey was acting like a *somate* already. He was letting Tris look after him. Make him pretty. Not that Drey wasn't already *pretty*, but he never dressed pretty.

Tristol's hair flattened in horror – was that a *hole* in one of Drey's socks? The man was a menace to himself.

"Shall we get noodles?" asked the big human, obviously unaware of the hole.

Tris tore his horrified gaze away from the sock in question and nodded. Together they padded over to a stall that specialized in pan-Asian cuisine. Tris got the gooey Singapore ones that he loved with egg and bits of unidentifiable (but tasty) meat. Drey got the Thai-style big flat ones with lots of vegetables.

Tris had forgotten his chopsticks again.

Drey pulled out a spare pair from his shirt pocket and handed them over without comment.

Tris telescoped them out and tried not to cry.

Drey must have collected the chopsticks when he went home to change clothing that morning. Even with the stress of his job and this new murder investigation and lack of sleep, Drey had remembered that Tris was forgetful. Drey had thought of him and *brought him chopsticks*. Was there ever a better *somate* in the whole universe? Drey was taking *care* of him and helping him to eat, not to mention preventing Tris the embarrassment of having to ask, again, for a spare set of chopsticks from the stall. That always caused the cook to chuckle and say something a little insulting about Tris being flighty.

Then Drey nearly exploded Tristol's heart by saying, "Give 'em back to me when you're done, baby, and I can keep 'em for you. Then it won't matter if you keep forgetting."

"You are *amazing*. I will find you the prettiest best socks on the whole space station," replied Tris, scooping up noodles with Drey's chopsticks with something close to exultation puffing up his hair.

Drey asked him some particularly odd questions as they ate lunch. Mostly about the nuances of galoi culture, and why Anisoi Ureeya might act the way he had. Tris tried to be as forthcoming as possible. He made certain to tell of his speculation regarding connection between captain and *isoga* guard. Although she was not very attractive. Still, there was no accounting for taste – look at Drey's socks. *No, do not look.*

Finished with the noodles, they were heading back toward Tristol's quarters by mutual and unspoken consent, when Mr Churig hailed Tris.

"What you doing out and about during daylight shift, kid?"

"It is *awfully* bright," agreed Tris.

"And why you got no shoes on?" The human's eyes shifted to Drey. "Detective?"

"Second date," explained Tris, jovially.

"Socks is some alien thing?"

"Yes," said Tris, pleased with himself. *I am mastering human deception and sarcasm and silliness, all at once!*

Drey was looking at him with sparking brown eyes and evident approval.

"You're a brave man, detective." Mr Churig was shaking his head and making a tut-tutting noise.

"For taking off my shoes?"

"For attempting to date this one. Tris, you said you'd come look at my cleaning unit. Do you have a moment?" Tristol's neighbor's voice was plaintive.

For some reason the elderly human was convinced that by virtue of Tristol being galoi, he would have advanced engineering knowledge. He was always asking Tris to help him *fix* things. Mostly human mechanized things that Tris himself never used. Let alone understood. But Tris was game to try.

"I will do my best, Mr Churig. What is broken today?"

The human waved them both into his abode. Which was arranged much like Drey's, only with a great deal more stuff piled everywhere.

Mr Churig pointed to some kind of large cleaning unit in his kitchen.

Tris approached it warily.

"Tris," whispered Drey, who obviously understood the seriousness of the situation, "are you good at repairing appliances?"

"No, but Mr Churig thinks so highly of me. I do not want to disappoint him." Tristol looked hopefully at Drey.

"Are you good at it?"

Drey flinched and shook his head. "The only thing I'm handy with is a com-unit. Which I use to call someone professional in to fix whatever's broken."

Tris nodded gravely. "I do not think Mr Churig knows how to use a com. He seems to prefer to yell at people in the hallway instead."

"Baby, I think that's just because he's ornery and cheap."

"Drey! That is not nice."

Drey snorted. "All right, what's going on with this thing, then?"

They cracked open the cleaning unit. It was one of those multipurpose ones, basically designed to clean whatever was put into it, from clothes to chopsticks to maybe even human younglings. Although Tris really did not know how humans cleaned their young – perhaps they waited until maturity? The ones in the park always seemed awfully grubby.

Judging from Mr Churig's quarters, he had never actually used his cleaning unit before. Perhaps because it had always been broken?

Tris crawled inside the thing and poked about, which resulted in it covering him with yellow bubbles.

That seemed to satisfy Mr Churig, who insisted that bubbles were what had been missing. Now that Tris had gotten them going again, all would be well.

Drey took that as an opportunity to escape. He dragged Tris out of the machine and then out of the apartment. "Come on, baby, let's get back to yours before anything else goes wrong."

"Do you not need to protect your feet inside shoes?" Tris was confused. The socks were a good joke but maybe they should just go shopping – then Tris could pick new shoes for Drey now, before his feet got damaged.

"Eventually. First I need back inside you. If you're up for it?"

"Oh, yes, please." Tris forgot all about shoe shopping. Which was pretty significant, since it was his favorite activity.

Well, *second* favorite activity.

Drey pounced on him the moment Tris sealed the door to his chambers. The big human folded them both down into Tristol's nest, making himself part of the mattress so Tris was draped over him in breathless wonder.

"There is something to be said for having one's bed right there at the door."

"You like my nest?"

"I love it, baby. It's so welcoming and bold and pretty."

"Not like poor Ooloi Villisol."

"His place did seem a little sad. Wait, that has meaning?"

"The sadness? Yes. A *loga's* nest is a reflection of a state of being." Tris gestured around them. "This is my statement of freedom, and pleasure and happiness. A little fear perhaps, there in the upper corners, and some loneliness in the shading. After all, this is decorated only with my own color palette."

"So when you suggested adding my colors, that means a significant mental shift for you?"

Tris could tell Drey had his detective brain working. He did not mind. He was being cradled, close, and Drey was all hard arousal under him – that side of things would progress soon enough. If Drey wanted to talk about nesting, Tris was delighted to do so.

"Emotional shift, more than mental. But yes. If you stay, you would become part of my nest, as you are part of my life. Ooloi Villisol did not have that."

"Would he paint his walls for lovers?"

"No. Nesting is for more than sex. I may have been hasty to speak of changing my shades so soon, by human standards, but you did say you wanted to maybe keep me."

"What's hasty?" Drey shrugged, still holding him tight.
"I've wanted to *keep you*, as you say, since I first saw you.
I just didn't think it was possible. I thought all galoi were
promiscuous. Now I know what can be, I'd be honored if
you incorporated my colors onto your walls."

Tris caught his breath and could not stop his hair from
writhing in wonder.

"Tris, this may not be the right time, but I think it's
important. Why are you *zyga*? Why are you a criminal in
the minds of your people?"

Tristol had been expecting such a question. Drey was
an upstanding human, a detective, a law-abider. He would
want to know why Tris was a reject. And if they were
considering *somate,* Drey also had a right to know.

"I refused *gamein*."

"You didn't want kids?"

Tristol's hair folded down. It was such a
*awful*sickening* thing to admit. His whole function as a
*loga* was to produce progeny. To birth life. Yet he did not
want young. He had never wanted them. He had known
that from the moment he became *loga*. From the moment
he knew he preferred to copulate with *antiga*. He had
known even then that he did not want the consequences of
that preference.

"I did not. I do not. I am sorry if that impacts us. Do
you want young, Drey, have I ruined all of it?"

"No, baby, I never wanted kids either. But it's not a big
deal to humans. There are plenty of those who do. And
being gay makes that choice kinda easy for me. I mean I
could've adopted, but yeah, I really don't care. My sister
has six. She's crazy for them."

"Six younglings!" Tris was amazed. "That is a great
many!" *And to raise them yourself, without creche or*
isoga*?*

"And three husbands, which she always jokes is a bit
like having nine children total. Agricultural planet,

combined with an innate love of being pregnant. There are some women like that, I suppose. I don't get it myself. So that's it, your great sin, saying no to children?"

Tris shook his head. "Saying no to *gamein*. Every *loga* owes the galoi three live births."

"Wait, what?" Drey had a very funny expression on his face, but at least he wasn't pushing Tris away. He held him close and his big hands were smoothing down Tristol's hair and back and ass, repetitively. As if Tris were a large version of Mister Montiguous and Drey was petting him from head to tail.

Tris sat up abruptly. "Oh, no! I need to go feed and play with Mister Montiguous! I have not yet told him he is a *wonderful feline creature* today. I am a failure at cat maintenance."

"Forget the cat for just a moment, Tris. Are you saying *gamein*, for you, means three pregnancies?"

"Of course. I am *loga*."

"You can *get pregnant*?"

Tris did not understand the confusion. "I am *loga*."

"But you're male. You have a cock, I don't—" Drey sat up too.

Tris was in his lap now and disinclined to move away from the human warmth, so he swiveled around to sit facing his confused *somate* and wrap both his legs about Drey's waist. "My penis is a vestigial sex characteristic, like your nipples." He tweaked one of the nipples in question.

Drey gave one of his lovely low moans and shuddered a bit. "Stop that, I'm trying to understand here. But you're classified as male."

"*Male loga*. That is my gender. You thought I was male like humans are male? No, the closest to that is *antiga*. *Antiga* are the ones who can inseminate, *loga* give birth."

"And *isoga*?"

"Ah, you want to know what *isoga* do biologically in

conjunction with procreation? They nurture. Our young are born very small, underdeveloped by human standards, as galoi have a much shorter gestation period than humans." Tris made the shape of a galoi joey, two hands cupped together.

Drey's face was all scrunched, which could mean disgust or confusion. "I suppose they would have to be quite small, if you birth it out of where I'm thinking you birth it out."

Tristol's hair vibrated in amusement. "Yes. Galoi birth is much less painful than human. Because our young are so tiny. It makes more sense to me. Your species seems to do it the hard way. Then again, it works so well for you, I suppose you can not complain."

"So, *isoga*?"

"Ah, they have a pocket, called the *issillib.*" Tris gestured to his bellybutton area. "It is like a seam or a pouch that stretches open when needed. They also lactate and feed the young, once the *issillib* is in use."

"Both *male* and *female isoga* have this?"

"Yes."

"And they're responsible for rearing children until they hit puberty?"

"Until they mature and acquire gender. Yes. Although, obviously, not inside the *issillib* all that time. That would be ridiculous. Once the infant is weaned and mobile, the *isoga's* primary duties are absolved and the infant is given to the creche for life education."

Drey was still looking funny-faced and scrunchy. Tris wished, for the first time, that Drey had proper hair so Tris could tell exactly what he was feeling.

"*Gamein* is this cultural mandate that *antiga* must create three lives, *loga* must birth them, and *isoga* carry them?"

Tris was delighted that Drey understood. "Yes, Drey, exactly. Very well done. Good boyfriend!"

"Baby, you don't need to treat me like the cat. Still, that's way complicated. No wonder your species is dying out."

"It is true. Although galoi do not speak of it so openly."

"Oh, fuck. I'm sorry, baby. I was trying to be funny."

"But galoi *are* dying out. We have had mass population decrease for almost four hundred years. We are relatively long-lived, by comparison to humans, but still it is catching up to us. Despite *gamein,* we are still steadily losing numbers. Very few can satisfy *gamein*, you see? There are fewer and fewer *loga* and *antiga* being born, and more and more *isoga*. Now even those births are rare. Some *loga* spend their entire adult lives pregnant, producing an endless series of non-viable offspring. Just to satisfy *gamein,* so they may be free to find *somate*."

"That's fucking fascist. You aren't allowed to marry or have a life until you've given three living children to the state?" Drey was wearing an expression Tris knew well – shocked offense.

Tris shrugged – that was good enough for comprehension. "Yes. Drey, are you *gobsmacked*? You look *gobsmacked*."

"And most of them will be stillborn? So *loga* just have to keep trying and trying?"

Tris nodded against Drey's chest.

"Oh fuck, baby, is that what happened to you? Is that why you left?"

"No, but it was my future."

"So you refused?"

"Not only for that reason."

Drey jerked suddenly. "Oh shit, Tris, you have a womb!"

"Well yes, sort of, as humans understand it."

"Could I have gotten you pregnant last night?"

Tris couldn't help it, his hair shook in laughter. "No. You are not *antiga*. And I would need to be in estrus. So far as I am aware, humans and galoi are not cross-species-compatible. You are welcome to try as much as you like, though."

"You're sure?"

"*Loga* have a seal to their wombs. Estrus is required to release the seal, and the *antiga's* barb is required for insemination. Much as I adore your penis, Drey, it is not barbed. And I have not experienced a heat since leaving Gal."

"Christ. Okay then. That's one less worry dealt with. Fuck, baby, I never thought I'd have a pregnancy scare, a gay man of my age."

"Is it that easy for human women to get inseminated? I mean, I knew human males were always fertile. But your females do not go into estrus? They are always able to get pregnant? That is remarkable! No wonder humans overpopulate the galaxy."

"Very funny, Tris. So, you refused to have three kids and the galoi kicked you off your home planet and no longer acknowledge your existence?"

"Yes. Basically." Tris didn't really have the words, not in galactic standard, for what *zyga* was like. The choice, the compulsion, to refuse to give life. It was as strong as a sexual preference, as gender identity, to him. And, he had always assumed, to other *zyga*. To give up everything, to leave one's culture and never return to it – it was not really a choice at all. Everyone misconstrued that. Even the galoi.

"Why do they let *zyga* go? Why not just trap you and force you? Or kill you as bad examples."

"The galoi are alien, Drey, but we are not evil. Our history has always had *zyga*, even before we had space travel. *Zyga* were exiled to islands or ocean vessels or some other remote location. We do not galoi life, Drey. Not even for us aberrants who refuse to procreate. How does that make sense? It only decreases the population by one more galoi. Our scientists believe *zyga* is a genetic aberration. Because the *zyga* not only deny function, but thrive in exile. We are the travelers, diplomats, and negotiators of our species. We are open-minded, we understand others, we understand aliens. It was *zyga* who united the planet, moving from one continent to the next. *Zyga* bring change and evolution through absence. We are the explorers and the ambassadors. We have purpose, even in exile."

"I noticed you seem to know everyone in Zone 3, all your neighbors, all the hawker cooks. You're friends with everyone and everyone loves you. It was a little maddening when all I wanted was for it to be me, but I suppose I could share your affection so long as I can keep your heart."

"I am *zyga* but I still want a *somate*. I would stay with you forever, if you wanted."

"I still can't believe they not only let you go, but actively ignore and reject you."

"There are not so many *zyga* for it to concern Gal as a whole. To bleed out so few? It is better to concentrate on trying to determine why birthrates are plummeting and why genders are narrowing. *Zyga* are treated as we always have been treated, only we are sent into space now instead of out to sea."

Drey was solid and warm against him, still petting him.

Tris writhed experimentally. Delighted when Drey's body responded by hardening further with desire. "This is all acceptable to you, Drey? My history? My state of being? My biology?"

"Strangely, yeah. I still believe you're the sexiest man I've ever met, *zyga* or *loga* or galoi or human. Thinking about your internal organs is a bit odd, but I don't have to think about them."

"I also have two stomachs."

"Equally weird. But as you can tell, I've not stopped finding you attractive." Drey rolled his hips up and that big penis, that fit so deep and perfect even without a barb (*especially* without a barb), was hard and hot against Tristol's ass.

He wiggled in delight and Drey groaned for him.

Then the big human went perfectly still, just when Tris thought they would finally be moving on from talking to fucking. "Did you say *two stomachs*?"

"Yes, Drey."

"So, the vomit?"

"Bile is only born in the first stomach, which means the poison must have been an unusually strong and fast-acting one. Because the first stomach is stronger and meant specifically to break down poisons and prevent bad stuff from entering the bloodstream."

"So there should be remnants of whatever poisoned him in the vomit?"

"Yes, Drey, that is likely."

Drey got even tenser. "Oh, fuck!" He tapped his ear-com, not releasing Tris, but clearly needing to contact dispatch.

Tris waited, passive and happy just to be in his arms.

"Patch me to the lab. Joel? … Yeah, dude, how's it floating? … You got that sample I sent in? … Yeah, poison … Oh you think? … I'm not copping attitude, I trust ya. It's only that I need you to run a pregnancy test on it, too … Yeah, *I know* the victim's male. He could still be pregnant. It's alien and complicated. Just see what you can do … Yeah, no I've no idea what galoi pregnancy hormones look like. Would it help if you had another male of the same biology for a baseline?"

Tris knew what was coming.

"Okay, we'll be there in ten minutes." Drey tapped off.

"Could you not have said twenty minutes and fucked me first?" Tris wondered, knowing he sounded whiny.

"Aw, baby, I'll make it up to you. After we get back I'll let you fuck me for a bit before I rail you."

Tris had never gotten to fuck anyone before. He considered whether he liked that idea, then thought about how warm Drey would be, because *human*, and how tight, because *male* human.

"After all, your cock comes pre-lubed. I bet you feel amazing."

*True.* The pre-lubed penis in question jumped and leaked at the idea, so apparently Tris did indeed like it. *I am so very perverted and ill-suited to staying on Gal. I am glad I left.*

"You said *zyga* were explorers, yeah? This is uncharted territory for you."

Tristol's hair floated upward at the thought that he would get to do something sexual that no other *loga* had ever done. That *definitely* turned him on.

"Yes, Drey," *somate,* "we will go give the lab human my fluids and then we will come back here and I will do what no *loga* has ever done before."

Drey grinned. "That's my brave boy!"

Drey examined his own psyche.

*My lover has female parts.*

He poked himself with the thought.

Turns out, he was fine with it. He'd dated an FTM once – hot as fuck, and he'd never once worried about the dude's internal organs. The fact that Tris had the capacity to give birth was fine. The reason for his exile was also fine. Drey hadn't lied when he'd said he didn't want children. His sister was doing her part to populate the galaxy with the next generation of Hastions. Drey might have to talk to Tris about fostering eventually. One of his nieces was wild to leave the farm and try station life. Drey couldn't blame her. But he'd had the feeling, given how friendly and welcoming Tris was with everyone, that hosting a teen at some point would be absolutely fine.

At the lab, Tris was sweet and calm about having his blood taken. The medic, a dorien, was delighted to have anything to pass along to the labbies to compare to the vomit sample.

"We really do need a baseline, small purple one. May I take a saliva and a stomach sample as well, please?"

"If you must," said Tris. "But only my first stomach. It will be mostly noodles, though. And I am *lavender*, thank you very much."

The dorien dipped xer silver head in acknowledgment and took the samples.

Tris did, however, insist that afterward Drey come along to feed and play with the damn cat. Then they went by Drey's place to pick up shoes and a change of clothes. Everyone's amusement at his socks notwithstanding, it was getting a little ridiculous for a member of station security to pussyfoot around like some kinda wanna-be ninja.

"We could stay here, if you like. In your home?" Tristol's purple eyes were big and intent – he was being polite.

"No, yours is nicer." Drey was quick to respond. Because it was. After being in Tristol's warm nest for only one night, his own apartment seemed pathetic – unfriendly and barren of life and interest.

Tris bounced a bit. "You like my nest?"

Drey, who was already learning Tristol's moods, scooped him up, held him close, and rubbed his neck with his beard. "It's perfect."

Tristol trilled at him.

By the time they made it back, however, daylight shift was ending and Drey's sleep cycle was all jacked up. He was utterly exhausted. Despite promises and exciting possibilities, he could hardly keep his eyes open.

"I'm sorry, baby, but I need to sleep."

"Then you sleep here. Stay. I will look after you."

Drey stripped (Tris helped) and then crawled into the nest.

Tris, who seemed to have boundless energy, bustled about quietly. He trilled softly to himself in evident delight.

He tucked Drey in, made sure he had a container of water resting on a nearby pillow, and turned off the lights. He took endless pleasure in simple acts of care – his noises almost as pleased as when he was being fucked, although fortunately not quite so loud.

"I'm good, baby," Drey said at last. "Come lie down with me? You must be tired too."

"I am. Thank you for inviting me." So formal, even as Drey grabbed and dragged Tris into his own nest.

He tucked the galoi in against him, careful not to scratch his sensitive hair with his beard. Instead he kissed the shifting locks softly. They floated down to wrap themselves around Drey's neck and shoulders.

"You look so pretty in my nest, Drey. And you are staying." Tristol's words were hushed, murmured, almost for his own benefit rather than Drey's.

Drey smiled. To think he'd thought this lovely man lacked constancy, was too flightily, when all along it seemed Tris wanted exactly what Drey wanted. Because Drey could never have imagined anything more perfect than fitting himself into this man's welcoming colorful world.

Although, to be honest, he could never have imagined bedding down on the living room floor inside an alien's nest, never mind the perfection of it.

Tris burrowed against him, his trills so soft as to be more a vibration. He still murmured words once in a while, but they were the lyrical musical words of his own language. Drey caught only one that he knew, which was "*somate*." He liked what he believed that meant and he wasn't scared of commitment. Tristol could call him *beloved* in his home language if he wanted to. *Please call me that.*

Drey fell asleep to the cool caress of silken strands, in a sea of soft purple, cradled by the alien music of Tristol's joy.

# THE 9TH CHAPTER

*No idioms for aliens*

Tris awoke to find himself warmer than usual. His hair was abnormally happy, content, and safe, *human*male* *somate*. Drey was still there and curled about him. Humans were such a lovely temperature, and Drey's heat-range was particularly pleasant, like a sunbeam.

The human may not be awake himself, but some parts of him were.

Tris went off on an exploring mission – he was *zyga*, after all. He let his hair play while he nuzzled Drey's chest and nibbled his nipples, then worked his way down to that big glorious penis.

He liked Drey's flavor very much – salty, musky, and a little bitter like the highly prized shellfish of the Sorree Coast mixed with *huerim,* his favorite comfort food. He also liked the way the more he licked, and the harder Drey got, the more his dark brown penis turned purple. *Purple! So perfect.*

Tristol knew Drey was awake when those large hands began to stroke through his hair. Wrapping about the strands, they tugged and twisted very gently. Tris ached and leaked and shuddered with small orgasms at the intimate touch.

Then he remembered what Drey had said yesterday. About his *loga* penis being perfectly designed (with all that slick cum) to penetrate a human male and he decided he wanted to try that.

Drey could tell that this was his intent because Tris poked him into rolling over and onto his hands and knees.

"You'll need to prep me, baby. I don't stretch like you do."

"How?" Tris demanded.

Drey chucked, reached back between his own legs to grab Tristol's penis, coaxing out another spurt of cum. Then he reached a little further and sank one finger into his hole.

Tris was fascinated. Then he thought he understood. A human would need to be stretched, like a *male isoga* who wanted to be fucked by an *antiga*. It wasn't a common pairing among galoi, but it wasn't taboo either. So Tris went to work, slowly but gently, first with one finger and then two and finally three, stretching Drey open enough to take him. Tris used liberally of his own excitement. Turns out it was unexpectedly hot doing this (and not just inside Drey's body). Tristol's penis just kept producing because he was so turned on. To take such care with his lover was very sexy – he understood why *isogas* liked it so much.

Finally Drey was groaning and shifting restlessly. "I'm ready, baby, I swear."

Tris trusted him. So he pulled back and positioned himself carefully. He slid his wet penis into Drey's tight heat. "Oh, wow."

Drey shook with amusement. "Like that, do you?"

It was just a little too constrictive and too warm, so Tris knew he could not thrust for long or he would get sore, but it also felt glorious and unlike anything he had ever experienced before. He experimented with thrusting and angles, finding one that caused Drey to jerk and moan. There was some spot he particularly liked, toward the front. Tris tried to press against it each thrust.

Drey made lovely noises when he was successful.

He curled himself down, so that the tips of the longest

of his hair strands could reach around and wrap themselves about Drey's large, neglected penis.

That caused his human to cry out and almost climax. Tris did not want that, because he wanted that big penis inside him again first, so he forced his hair to stroke Drey's nipples instead. Drey groaned in both pleasure and denial that the hair had moved away.

"Please, baby!" he begged nicely.

Tris whispered, "*Somate*," and pressed little kisses into the broad brown back beneath him.

All too soon it got too much. He ached with emptiness and frustrated need. He would love to do this again and Drey certainly seemed to enjoy it, but now he really wanted to be fucked. When Tris withdrew, Drey whimpered at the loss, but he also flipped onto his back readily enough.

Quick as he could, Tris gathered up cum from the head of his now incredibly sensitive penis, and smeared it down Drey's – *Purple! Yes!* – before climbing eagerly onto it.

Drey arched up off the nest and gasped as Tris sank down.

"Good that is so fucking good." Drey's voice was so low and deep it was almost an *isoga* sub-vocalization.

Tris was trilling his own pleasure, nearly nonstop now that he had Drey inside him where he belonged. He rose up and down, forcing the head to slam against the seal of his womb, buffeting himself exactly right for climax.

Before he lost himself in his own pleasure, though, he wanted to try something crafty. He tilted forward just a bit, wrapping one of the longest of his hair strands about his own penis, coating it in slick.

Then he reversed his posture, arching his spine backward, sinking down, and arching as far back as he could. He was flexible enough for it, as it turned out, and it drove Drey's penis exactly onto the right spot. It was so perfect, Tris had to ease up slightly to stop himself from full orgasm.

He reached down with his hair. Using every modicum of what was left of his control. He guided one long slick strand hard and deep into Drey's ass. It could not go very far, but it could crook to stroke Drey's erogenous point, closer to the opening and toward the front of Drey's body.

"Holy fuck, baby," yelled Drey and bucked under him, climaxing, almost unseating Tris. His hair strand slid out, having done its job. Tristol slid back down fully, and lost himself to pleasure, shuddering and throbbing with climax both inside and out, over and over until he was boneless.

When he recovered his senses, it was to find himself sprawled on top of Drey, still stuffed with slowly deflating human, blissfully happy.

Drey was saying, "How the fuck did you think to do that?" Petting his hair with total reverence. Like his hair was the most wonderful thing ever.

It is possible Drey was also trying to get the cum out of it.

Tris blushed to remember what he had done. It had been so very against *loga* nature, but it did seem to have worked.

"You liked it, though, right, Drey?"

"I fucking *loved* it, baby."

"You said I should explore."

"And you said you were good at it. You sure as fuck didn't lie."

Tris trilled and snuggled closer.

Drey's penis slipped out of him and his seed tricked after. Such an oddly pleasurable sensation, to be warm and used and given over. Like he had something of Drey's inside him. Also odd, to think that human females did not have a catch-seal and still managed to get pregnant.

Tris sighed. He supposed they would need to leave the nest soon.

Then Drey tensed and reached up to tap his ear. "Yeah?"

A long pause and then, "I'll be there asap … Yes, Joel,

Mr Zyga will be with me … How is that any of your business? … You wish! Considering what just happened, you *really* do wish … Fuck off, you're straight and he's mine … Yeah, yeah, see you in a bit."

Drey closed the com and shifted under Tris. Restless.

"I am yours?"

"You so fucking are. If you think after that I'm ever letting your ass go, you're insane. Your hair alone is a goddam gift to mankind, and I'm just selfish enough to keep it all to myself."

"Yes, Drey," said Tris. The hair in question tingling and lifting at such a profound compliment.

"But baby, we have to cleanse and get moving."

"You want me to go to the lab with you?"

"You can only be of help."

"I can? Oh, you are so good to me."

Tris lifted himself reluctantly off his big human, and they made their way, knees still a little shaky, to Tristol's small cleansing unit.

Joel was in top form when Drey and Tris showed up at the lab. For Joel, top form was basically just being an asshat.

Joel was a tall, floppy dude with hair so blond it was almost white, an oversized nose, and a wide mouth that was prone to oversized smiles and foul language.

He was also one of Drey's closest friends on the station.

"Dude, this vomit is so fucking cool." Joel looked up, noticed Drey, and started relaying information without even a greeting. Joel could never be bothered with niceties, especially if there was cool vomit around.

"Come take a look!" He flapped the two of them over.

"Joel, this is Mr Zyga. Tristol, this is Joel. He's a dick."

Tris looked the labbie up and down. "He *is* rather tall and skinny but he does not look *exactly* like a penis. He is pretty, like a penis, though. He is the first pale human I have seen with nicely matched hair."

Joel paused to stare at Tris. "Dude, you're fucking purple. I don't see how you can make a comment like that."

"But I am similar *shades* of purple, all of which are *lavender*. Have you considered dyeing your hair a peach color? It would go very nicely with your skin. Or perhaps a light blue, to match your eyes?"

Joel seemed a little startled by the fact that instead of talking about vomit they were talking about hair and eyes. Drey knew what that felt like. Hair-related incidents happened a lot around Tristol.

Drey figured it was up to him to get things rolling back in the correct direction. If Tristol started in on aesthetics and fashion advice, they'd be there half a shift and probably all end up shoe shopping together.

"The barf, Joel. The barf."

"Right, man. Fuck, Mr Zyga, you're a particularly weird little purple dude, aren't you?"

"*Lavender*," said Tris. His hair didn't seem to know how to react to Joel, alternating between wiggling at the tips, which Drey thought meant *curiosity*, to going quite stiff, which was *control*, to wilting a bit, which was *discomfort*.

Drey decided to try and smooth things over. "Don't take Joel seriously, baby. He's all *fuck-off, world* until something interesting is under his lens. So, vomit?"

"*Baby,* is it?" said Joel as he led Drey over to the scopes.

Joel flicked his middle finger and thumb at the vid and called up a whole mess of charts and graphs and images that meant nothing to Drey, but looked important.

Tristol tilted his head and pointed to one of the SEM backscatters. "That one is pretty."

"Joel?" pressed Drey.

"Your victim was killed by a plant. Not a plant that's in

our data system, but definitely a plant. Some of it's half-chewed. Here, look at this." He circled a finger and one of the images enlarged.

Drey glanced at Tris. "Those little white flowers on the ceiling of the boy's nest? They're toxic? If so, this could actually be an accident."

Tris shook his head. "No. *Alysigoss* will not kill a galoi. They taste bad, but they do not kill."

Joel interrupted. "Not *little*. The striations and material composition suggest a large petal or trumpet formation for the plant in question."

"Trumpet? Musical instrument?" queried Tris.

Joel continued without pausing. "Oh and not *white* either, more a pale purple color." He glanced at Tris, then corrected himself with great emphasis, "*Lavender* color and spotted with other purples like, oh, *violet*, and *amethyst*, and *plum*, and—"

Drey interrupted the litany. "Like those other flowers the galoi have in the main hallways, the ones for oxygen production rather than airflow."

Tris nodded back. "*Shillamith*. Those *are* poisonous. Quite deadly, actually. I am just accustomed to thinking of them as a part of the mechanics of a spaceship." His big eyes were wide and his hair was flat. "What kind of mind would turn what gives us breath into a weapon? That is not galoi, that is insanity!" He looked like he might cry.

Drey stroked one strand of Tristol's hair for comfort. An oddly sexual gesture now, after what Tris had done with that amazing hair earlier. Drey thought he must be the luckiest gay guy ever. Tristol brought new life to the concept of being *versatile* in bed. Or should Drey say *plumbed new depths* of that concept?

*Now I'm getting distracted.* "So we have our murder weapon. Uh, murder plant," said Drey. "Anything else?"

Joel pulled up a chart. "His last meal was mostly meat, something close to chicken."

"Isn't it always?"

"Don't interrupt my flow, dude. Where was I?"

"Chicken."

"Right. There's a mild alcoholic beverage present. Fermented but not fizzy. Some fruit or vegetable matter as well. Your victim ate a full meal right *before* he ate the poison plant."

"He'd just had dinner?" Drey frowned.

"Or lunch or whatever the aliens call it."

"Good to know."

Tris didn't say anything. He was watching Drey and Joel volley back and forth with wide, interested eyes. His hair was no longer flat and shivering, it had puffed up to what Drey had come to think of as its baseline state. A state that also represented Tristol at heart – excited and game to try.

"Tris, do galoi have onboard recording vids in common areas like we do in hawker centers?"

Tristol nodded at him. "Yes, Drey."

"So we might be able to get footage of where he was eating and who left with him right before he was killed?"

"Yes, Drey. But there will be *a lot* of footage. Galoi spend most of their time in communal nests. We only really sleep and fuck *somates* in private. And even that can be done communally."

"Horny little purple buggers, are you?"

"Be nice, Joel." Drey glared.

Tris didn't seem to take offense. "Horny is good. But I am still *lavender*, Mr Joel. *Lavender*."

Joel grinned at him.

Tris melted under the wide smile. "Oh! Mr Joel, you are handsome. I did not realize."

"He's straight," barked Drey, surprised at the surge of jealousy.

Tris nudged up to him, hair coiling around his arm. "It was an observation, not an invitation. You said you would keep me. Do you need me to wear an earring for you?"

"You two are talking rings already? Look, can we finish with the vomit? All this lovey-dovey shit is making me sick. And that'd mean even more vomit for me to deal with."

"You are unwell, Mr Joel? Sit down then, please."

"He's kidding, Tris. Go on, Joel, anything else?" The fucker did so like to be coaxed.

"Sorry, man, but that's about it. Nothing came up on your weird-ass dead-dude pregnancy test request. Even with Mr Zyga's help, I just didn't know what to look for. All I can say is, nothing was off compared to Mr Zyga's test results."

Drey noticed that Tristol didn't encourage Joel to call him by his first name. "I'll have to try to get that out of the galoi doctor, then."

Tristol said, "I am sorry, Mr Joel, but I have no physician's training myself, so I would never know what to look for in pregnancy either."

"It's alright, kid."

"I am small but not young, Mr Joel."

"How old are you, Tris?" It occurred to Drey to wonder. He did feel a bit like he was robbing the cradle. *Or I guess it would be robbing the creche.* Tristol's face was so pretty and his skin so smooth, he looked like he was in his twenties.

"In your human years, Drey? Let me calculate. Perhaps a hundred?"

Joel hooted at Drey's shocked expression. "You're porking a geriatric."

Tristol drew himself up as much as possible. "I am middle-aged, Mr Joel! Galoi live to about one hundred and sixty human years."

Drey had never been good at math. "So you're about the equivalent of forty?"

"Yes, Drey."

"Good. I too am the equivalent of forty. Now, Joel, are we done here?"

"Oh, we are *so* done. Dude, I got ammo on you for days. You're dating a purple – sorry, little dude, *lavender* – geriatric and you want to put a ring on it. Your ass is *mine* next pizza night."

Tristol's hair did something Drey had never seen before. It went stiff and straight out to the sides, then kinked like forked lightening.

He stepped forward and placed himself in front of Drey. "Tris? Are you... *angry*?"

Tristol had his arms out a bit as if braced protectively. Which was *absurd* because he was half Drey's weight and came from an entirely pacifist species.

Tristol's voice had even more of the musicality in it, like when he was speaking galoi. "*Human* male*untrusted* Joel. I convince you!" Tris paused, struggling for the right words.

Drey was amazed. Normally Tris had such a fantastic grasp of galactic standard, it was almost as if he were native-born, but suddenly it seemed to have deserted him.

Tris rebooted his rant. "*Human*male*untrusted* Joel, I assure you *human*male*somate*detective* Drey Hastion and *his ass* are *mine*!"

Joel backed away, shocked for once into seriousness. "Whoa there, little dude. My bad."

"Tris, baby, he means when we have our next friendship gathering that he's going to tease me about you."

Tris was not ready to be pacified. "Why? What is there to tease about? Why would he be mean to you, Drey, about me? This man is your friend?"

"Joel's actually alright, baby. He just *acts* like an asshole most of the time. He doesn't mean anything bad by it. He's planning to tease me because he knows how much I'm into you."

"And that is a joke?" The hair was still kinky.

"To Joel, everything is a joke. It's because I've not had a boyfriend since I moved here. It's affection. I think Joel is happy I've finally got someone. But he doesn't process it well, because he's all straight and shit, and he's probably lonely himself, so he teases me."

"This is normal human behavior?"

"Normal for Joel."

"I do not like it." Then suddenly Tristol's hair returned to its slightly wavy floating state. "Oh! You have not had a boyfriend before? I am the first one you wanted to keep? But that makes me *special*."

"You *are* special, baby."

Joel interjected at that. "Oh he's *special*, alright. Look, dudes, I'm getting queasy. You're really fucking sappy."

"Go away, Joel," said Drey, reaching for Tris. He figured he ought to kiss his boyfriend, reassure him, get his hair to go all puffy.

"This is my lab, you fucker. *You* go away. Don't you have a fucking crime to solve? Grope your weird purple boyfriend later."

Tristol received Drey's kiss as his due and then turned, hair now quite fluffy, and snuggled back against Drey. He glared at the lab tech. "You are a difficult person, Mr Joel. *Very difficult.*"

"Joel is advanced-grade human," said Drey, "Even we don't understand him half the time."

"May I attend this pizza night friendship gathering and observe the ritual teasing?"

"Sure you can, little dude." Joel's shoulders relaxed. Joel was prickly and sarcastic but he wanted to amuse, not offend. He'd prefer it if Tristol liked him.

"My name is Tristol," said Tris.

Drey let out a breath of relief. "You gonna graduate him from *human male untrusted* to something nicer?"

"Maybe after this pizza night friendship gathering event. So long as he really does not want your ass. It is a very nice ass. I want to keep it and play with it and stick my hair—"

"Okay!" Drey interrupted *that* right quick.

Joel was now gawking at Tristol's hair. "I *so* don't want to know."

Drey laughed. "Straight boy, you have no idea. And you really *do* want to know. Just find yourself your own fucking lavender alien."

With which parting shot Drey ushered Tris from the room.

"Drey!" Tris gasped at him once they were in the semi-privacy of the hallway. "That man is very impossible, is he not?"

"Very, baby. Hold on just a moment."

Drey dashed back into the lab.

"Test results, dude." He said to Joel's slumped back.

Joel's face was crestfallen. "Did I fuck it up for you? Man, I've never seen you that into a guy before."

He passed over the data button. Drey snapped it into his sleeve. The lab was on a closed network, so data transfer was crazy old-fashioned.

"You didn't fuck anything up, Joel. Tris is just sensitive. This thing between us is new and he's, you know, an alien and all. So we got shit to figure out."

"But you like him *a lot*, don't you?"

"I'm gonna marry him, Joel. If he'll have me."

"Fuck. It's the hair, right?"

"You have no idea."

"I'm still going with the experimental tech angle. If he was so smart and so useful that your planet let him out of *gamein* just to travel on this specific spaceship... That's a thing worth killing for."

Tris considered this. "It is a good working theory, Drey."

"Thanks, baby."

They were walking together back toward Zone 3.

Drey paused and tapped at his ear. "Yeah? Oh hi, boss ... Yeah, just been to the lab to collect the results. We know what killed him. Now we just need to find out who ... Mr Zyga is with me ... Hold on." He tapped the com-mute. "Honey, did you forget your com unit again?"

Tristol patted at his pockets. "Oh no! Yes, I did. Adjudicator Jones will be so upset. And during a work shift too. What must she think of me? I did not even report in this morning to tell her I was assisting you." He panicked. *Would she be mad at him?* Mostly Adjudicator Jones overlooked Tristol's sporadic distractive moments, but there were very important things going on right now. She might be angry.

"Okay, baby, hold on." He tapped his ear again. "Boss? Would you let Jones know that Mr Zyga is with me? ... Yeah, you can take that as the norm going forward. He's gonna stay with me. Or to be more precise, I'm gonna stay with him."

"Drey is *keeping* me," said Tris, loudly, because everyone should know this wonderful thing. He was hoping Drey's boss could hear him even through the earpiece. Also, maybe it would echo back down the hallway to that aggravating Mr Joel and show him what was *what*!

"Yeah, that's him. He's weirdly happy about it. Like I'm some kinda catch ... I think it's the reverse, too ... But I ain't gonna disabuse him of the notion ... Yeah, we're headed your way, unless— Hold up, boss, that's the Ambassador, I'm patching him in." Drey double-tapped his ear and said, "Ambassador Quinn? I have the security chief on-com as well. Is it time? ... Yessir ... No sir ... Yessir, he's with me .... Yeah, we're ready ... Tris might want to change clothes. Might want me to change clothes, too ... It seems like an important thing with the galoi ... Give us a few minutes, let them sweat it." He tapped off.

"They're apparently ready to try again. Maybe even play nice. The galoi captain reached out to the ambassador, audio only, of course, to say he has test results and that the doctor would be meeting with us to explain them."

Tris nodded, wondering at the possible hidden meanings. "That is good, Drey. We know that the doctor is also *female isoga*, like the guard. So expect her to be protective with her information. Cautious. Careful handling is called for. *Isoga* can be prickly."

"You'll be there to help me though, baby."

"I will? You still need me with you?" Tris felt almost floaty in relief. He did not want to say anything to Drey that might smack of lack of confidence, but he did not think Drey was ready to go among the galoi alone. Not yet, and possibly not ever.

"You're staying with me, baby, remember? That means on that spaceship. I'm not going aboard without you, that's for damn sure."

Tristol's hair puffed. "Oh, that is *good*. I want to help. I think I need to be there with you to do that."

"Exactly. But first, should I wear something other than the uniform? Is there any advantage in a different color?"

Tristol looked him up and down. "Not yet. When you are closer to solving the crime, we might need to force matters, visually speaking. But not now. Do you own a white suit, by any chance, Drey?"

"I do. Might be a bit tight. I had it for my sister's wedding twenty-odd years ago. But I think it still fits."

Tris nodded. Inside he was wincing at the idea.

Of course Drey would have something white. It was a very daring color with much ritual significance for humans. It was used for everything from weddings to shrouds to religious robes. Tris was sad to learn that purple was not particularly important to humans. It had been, once a long time ago. But even black or red had more meaning these days. Purple was thought of as special and wealthy and occasionally dramatic, but not particularly *significant*. Lavender was considered rather trivial. Tris intended to somehow fix that. But *white?* He shuddered. White was *awful!* But so powerful with its ugly brightness. So sharp. He supposed humans with their love of contrast, might find it appealing.

"Save it for later, Drey. Your uniform will do for now."

"And you're okay in that?"

Tris was wearing a mauve suit, warm-toned, complementary but not matching his own lavender skin. It was one of his least favorites, but it was a statement of solidarity. Should any of the galoi on that ship deign to notice him, they would know what the color meant.

"No, I put this on intentionally this morning, knowing you might let me return to the ship with you, to help."

"That's the color of Ooloi Villisol's skin, isn't it?"

"Almost exactly."

"You're making a statement of allegiance?"

"Should any galoi actually look at me, yes. We are both *loga* and they killed him. Someone killed him. Someone is insane on that ship. I want them to know Ooloi Villisol has an advocate. Even if I gave no strand and it is only a *zyga* on his side. Even if he has already died and his hair collapsed without memory."

"You're amazing, baby, you know that?"

Tris trilled at the compliment. How did he ever get so lucky as to catch the interest of this big wonderful human male? That he could make Drey happy just by being himself, just by doing what came naturally.

They made their way to the galoi spaceship.

This time, no one was waiting for them in the hallway except a security detail. The soldiers let them inside without question, nodding at Drey in solidarity. Clearly, they had been told what to expect. They had on the same color uniform as Drey. *Solidarity indeed.*

Anisoi Ureeya met them with his *isoga* guard at the top

of the ramp and around the corner, exactly as before. This time, however, they were led the other way in the ship, coiling upward away from the residence warrens and the enclosed spaces.

"Is it built using fractal mathematics?" Drey asked Tris.

But Anisoi Ureeya answered. "I do not know the term, human detective."

"Neither do I," whispered Tris.

Drey only shrugged. "I wouldn't know how to explain it, but your ship does kinda look like a big iridescent shell from one of those huge sea snails of Moritic Core."

"Is that a good thing?" Anisoi Ureeya asked.

Drey looked between him and Tris for a second – finally he said, "It's a very pretty sea snail."

"Then it is a good thing." The captain's gorgeous violet hair puffed a bit in pride.

Tris felt his own hair smooth in response, a compliment well-received could be nothing but a relief.

Moving through the familiarity of the galoi ship did not hurt as much on this second visit. Tris was, however, oddly upset by the *shillamith* flowers. They had so recently been his favorite. He always loved the way they looked against his skin, when he wove them into a wreath to wear about his neck. Now they seemed sinister, both life-giving and life-taking.

The ship's doctor was waiting for them in an empty room.

Given how different human quarters were from galoi ones, Tris made sure to explain the significance of the barren space to Drey. "This is not the doctor's quarters, nor is it her sick bay, nor is it her lab. This room has been purged of its function, probably with you in mind."

Drey nodded. "I'm not surprised, but thanks for the info, baby."

There was also no nesting material to sit upon. In fact there was nothing. The doctor just stood there, waiting for them alone, without color around her.

She was *isoga,* all right. Not quite as big as the one guarding Anisoi Ureeya, but still bigger than Tristol, and tough-looking. She had the same taste as the guard, for she wore black and silver rings in her preference ear. *No studs in her bonding ear, though.* So she was not Anisoi Ureeya's *isoga.* Tris was suddenly convinced that the guard was indeed his somate. It was unlikely that there were any other *antiga* aboard to have given the guard her black stud. Tris had forgotten how limited spaceships were. He was too accustomed to space station life.

He leaned against Drey's warmth and whispered, "The guard *isoga*? She is definitely Anisoi Ureeya's spouse."

Drey didn't question how Tris suddenly knew this, only nodded his understanding and acceptance.

"What can you tell me about this doctor, baby?"

Tris said, "She is—"

"You may ask me the questions, *human*male* detective*, not your *zyga.*" The doctor's mastery of galactic standard was good, Tris thought. Although not as good as his or the captain's. Perhaps she had worked a trade ship? She was also looking directly at him. Here was an *isoga* who needed to *know* things rather than just *believe* them. To her, Tristol's nothingness actually existed. She might even realize that it could be a tool to help the humans.

Anisoi Ureeya, behind them, made a hiss of objection.

Tris turned to look at him.

The *isoga* doctor swiveled her head as well and spoke in rapid galoi. "Anisoi Ureeya *antiga*once lover*now-maybe?-friend*trusted-enough* you can not order *instruct*demand*insist-in-public* that I ignore *not see*not hear*not know* what you yourself claim *insist-to-yourself-and-others* does not exist *riskriskrisk.*"

Tris translated the galoi swiftly for Drey. "She is saying that she insists on seeing me as *here,* even though I am *zyga,* even though the captain does not acknowledge me.

She understands that I am a risk to the integrity of this ship, and that I am an instrument, possibly a weapon, being used by humans against galoi. Oh and she and Anisoi Ureeya have had sex in the past. She trusts him somewhat. He does not entirely trust her."

"You got all that from one short sentence?"

"I told you galoi was an incredibly complex and precise language."

Drey nodded.

The doctor was looking at him again.

Drey spoke to her. "Your hair isn't covered, doctor. Interesting choice. And you may call me *detective*."

"I trust myself to control my emotions, *detective*. And I am Belloi Rissib. You have met Anisoi Ureeya. The stiff at his side, protective as a creche queen, is Belloi Froleb."

Anisoi Ureeya hissed at her again. A totally justified hiss! Tristol was on his side in that matter. The *isoga* had no right to name another galoi to an alien!

"It is the way humans do these things." Belloi Rissib was unruffled. "It is called *introductions*. I thought they were here to help us?" She returned her gaze to Drey. "So, you want to know what I found?"

He arched one dark brow at her. "All you labbies are the same, aren't you? Gotta be coaxed. Yeah, I want to know. Please tell me of your scientific brilliance."

Belloi Rissib's hair puffed a tiny bit. *Stupid* isoga, *that is not a compliment, that is human sarcasm being applied, plus bonus eyebrow action. I understand it,* Tris crowed to himself, *yet the other* galoi *do not!* He felt special.

Belloi Rissib reported her results. "He ingested a *shillamith* flower and that is what killed him."

Drey grunted. "Anything else?"

"No."

"Did you run a pregnancy test?"

"No. That is intrusive. And why would I? All the *logas* aboard are on estrus bind."

Drey looked at him. "Tris, what does that mean?"

"Heat suppressants, Drey. They keep *loga* from becoming fertile and going into estrus."

Drey grunted again. "Birth control. How's it administered?"

Belloi Rissib and Tris both answered him. "Pill."

"So he might have missed some, be at risk? I take it you *can* run a pregnancy test, doctor? Even if it's intrusive? After all, he's unlikely to feel it anymore, he's dead."

Belloi Rissib could not control her hair at that. It quivered slightly.

Tris felt his own shake a little in response.

"That would require an *autopsy*, detective. Galoi testing for pregnancy is surgical."

"So?"

"We do not cut into the flesh of our dead as if they were food," explained Tristol. Swallowing down bile at the very idea.

Drey shrugged. "Give us the body. Tell us what to look for. We'll figure it out for you."

Belloi Rissib's hair shot out at that. Stiff, horrified.

Anisoi Ureeya snapped. "Under no circumstances would we allow one of our people to leave this ship, dead or alive. Why do you need to know something we have already told you is not possible?"

Drey sighed. "Because most murders are committed by those close to the victim. Intimates like spouses, lovers, or family members. Galoi don't seem to have family, and Ooloi Villisol was unwed, so *lovers* is the most likely possibility. Pregnancy, particularly an unwanted or unexpected one, is motive."

"You speak of humans killing humans, detective. We are galoi. We do not even have a word for *murder*."

"So Tris has told me. And yet, you patently have a murderer aboard your ship, so perhaps you might need to invent that word. Meanwhile, I have to go with what I know. And what I know are human murders. Therefore, that's what I'm using as a basis for investigation. Killing like this is usually a crime of passion or reputation. So let's find out if our boy has a bun in his oven, okay?" He looked intently at Belloi Rissib.

Tris was confused and his hair showed it. "Drey, cooking bread is for later!"

Drey cleared his throat. "Right, no idioms for aliens. Just find out if he was pregnant, okay?"

The *isoga* nodded. "Very well, detective. You wait here."

She stood and left the room.

The other two galoi followed her.

The moment they were alone, Drey gathered Tris close into a hug. "You doing okay, baby?"

Tris nodded against him, obviously pleased by the comfort. "It was weird to be *noticed*."

"Yeah, I thought it might be."

"You really think Ooloi Villisol is pregnant?"

"I think it very likely." Drey didn't know why, but his instincts had kicked in. It didn't matter to him that these were aliens, he trusted his instincts. He'd been a detective for twenty years. And this was not his first alien murder investigation. In the end, killing always came down to procreation or survival, ideology or despair. For all species.

"Are we truly alone in here?" he asked Tris.

"No. They will be watching us remotely and listening."

Drey sighed and cuddled him closer, bending to whisper very softly into his ear. "They're all so much less gentle and happy and excitable than you, baby."

"They are *isoga* and *antiga* and I am *loga*."

"Would our victim have been like you then, bubbly and sweet?"

"Yes, but not exactly, of course. We are different people, but in general similar. *Logas* are inclined to have what humans call *sunny dispositions*." Tris said it like he was very fond of the term.

Sooner than Drey expected (considering surgery was involved), the doctor returned. Her hair was still under strict control but it seemed even stiffer, as if she were really having to force it to stay still.

She was also alone.

"So?" Drey demanded.

She gave a funny low rumble sound, then said, "Pregnant. How did you know, detective?"

"They're always fucking pregnant." Drey sighed and rubbed his eyes.

He kept hold of Tris, though, with his other arm, because Tris would need it. And maybe he did, a little, too.

Tris gave a high keening trill and folded against Drey.

Drey rubbed circles into his lower back. Poor baby, he identified a little too closely with the victim.

"You are lovers," said the doctor, watching them. "I did not know humans and galoi could be intimate." She looked away then, pensive, up at the misty chiming ceiling flowers. "That is good. Good for a *zyga* to have someone, even if it is only physical. Can you achieve full orgasm?" This was clearly a clinical question and it was directed at Tris.

She really didn't care about his outcaste state.

"Hey, now!" Drey cautioned.

But Tris raised his head from Drey's chest, forgetting his pain in annoyance. "*Somate!*" he hissed at the doctor. "Mine!"

"Ah." She held up a hand, pressed all her fingers to her thumb and twisted it slowly in the air, opening it flat at the last moment. "I do not understand, but I accept." It smacked of ritual.

Tris subsided in his arms.

Drey decided to move them back onto the subject of murder. "Can you identify the father? Uh," he paused, realizing they probably didn't use that word. "The sire?"

"The *antiga*," corrected Tris.

Of course, there was only one gender that could produce sperm. Thus all fathers were, by default, *antiga*.

The doctor looked uncomfortable. "Even if we had such a thing, I do not need a test for it. There is only one *antiga* aboard this ship and we have been out of contact with other galoi for a long time."

"The captain," said Drey.

"Anisoi Ureeya," said Tris at the same time.

"Naughty boy," added Drey. "I bet Belloi Froleb is going to give him an earful."

Both the galoi looked at Drey as if he was crazy.

"Why would she do that?" wondered Tris.

"Because he's stepping out on her."

"Stepping out?" Tris looked around the room and then pointed toward the hull and outer space.

"Sleeping around. Fucking someone not his wife. Or, erm, *wives*, spouses," Drey added. "He is married to Belloi Froleb, right?"

The doctor nodded.

"Well, good," said Drey, feeling something like optimism for the first time since he came aboard the spaceship, "we've got us three pretty good suspects, then."

Tris was still clearly mystified – his hair was all over the place. "We do?"

"Belloi Froleb, Anisoi Ureeya, and their other spouse. You said that would be a *female loga*, right? So, suspects."

"But why would they care enough to kill?"

"Well, the two ladies because Ureeya was cheating on them, and Ureeya because he had reason to want to cover it up. He had to do something. After all, pregnancy has a way of becoming public knowledge eventually."

Tris and the doctor clearly didn't follow his reasoning.

"He was not cheating," insisted Tris. "Cheating would be to copulate with a *female isoga* or a *female loga*. Ooloi Villisol was neither."

Drey balked. "Well, fuck. You only think of it as cheating if it's with someone of the gender you're already married to? That's messed up." Suddenly nervous, he looked intently down at Tris. "Baby, I would think you cheated if you fucked *anyone* else, okay? Male, female, neuter, both, or neither. Understand?"

"But I only ever wore one earring, Drey, and you fulfill the black ring for me, so yes, of course I understand."

Drey let out a long breath of relief.

The doctor was watching them with interest. "Will you wear his stud, *zyga*? As if you were somehow one of us again?"

Drey didn't think her words were intentionally cruel, but Tristol's hair deflated.

"He can wear whatever he damn well pleases, it's no concern of yours," he barked at her, losing, it must be admitted, a little of his professional cool.

She shook her hair at him in a galoi laugh. "Detective, you are as protective as an *isoga* and as arrogant as an *antiga*. No wonder this *zyga* found you."

"Mine," said Tris again, but this time it was just a statement, not a defense.

"Yes, I see that, but he does not wear your stud either. And he is very attractive. How do you know he does not want to try a little *isoga* aggression in his bed?"

*Is she flirting with me?* Drey could feel his eyebrows going up nearly to his hairline.

The doctor moved toward him, hips undulating seductively.

*Oh holy shit, she is flirting.*

"Uh, whoa there, ma'am." Drey was flustered. "Belloi Rissib. I'm so fucking gay I shit sparkles, and so totally taken that the idea of cheating makes me shit bricks, and thus completely not interested."

This didn't seem to have much of an effect on the *isoga*. Although Tris was craning his head to look at Drey's ass thoughtfully.

Drey scrabbled for something that would work to shut the *isoga* down. "White fucking earring, okay, lady?"

"You humans and your profanity." She had her hand on his arm and the other one was going to pet his head.

"A little help here, Tris baby?"

"*Somate!*" yelled Tris at her, and he was back to standing defensively in front of Drey, as he had in the lab with Joel. Only his hair was perfectly civilized, so he wasn't really that upset.

The doctor backed away, though her hair was doing that galoi shaking-laugh thing.

"She's not serious, is she?"

Tris looked back at him, still defensive. "She would fuck you, happily. She has the black earring as well as the silver. You are as *antiga* to her as you are to me."

"You saying, I'm her type?"

"Yes, Drey."

"But you aren't as mad as you were with Joel?"

"Joel is human, your own species, how could I compete with that? Plus I know you do not want to fuck females." Tris looked suddenly very smug. "You want to fuck me."

"Yeah, baby, I do. So can we all just calm down? Fucking hell, your lot shifts to sex quickly." He turned back to the doctor. "Look, no sex, okay, Belloi Rissib? Now, I don't care what you or Tris think, I need to interview the captain and his, what's-it-called? *Mycota*? Yeah. All of them."

"But they will not care that Anisoi Ureeya was sleeping with the fifth gender, when they are four and two," Tris protested.

"Oh, they cared, baby. They always care."

The doctor looked complacent. "It will not be hard to talk to Anisoi Ureeya. Also, I suspect Belloi Froleb will want her say as well, once they have both recovered from their grief."

"Grief?"

"At the death of both the *loga* and his young. But I doubt you will be allowed to interview Ooloi Marrel. Belloi Froleb is very protective of her. Ooloi Marrel birthed four live births, *four of them*! And two of those became *loga*! She is a national asset."

Drey was quite interested in this information. "Were they Anisoi Ureeya's kids?"

"Of course not!"

Tris whispered, "*Loga* never carry the young of their *somate*."

"Okay then. Has he any live births to his credit?"

"Yes, the requisite three. All became *isoga*, sadly."

"You belittle your own gender?" The doctor was a bit of a conundrum.

"There are too many of us."

"And what gender was the unborn child of our victim?"

The doctor looked disgusted and didn't answer.

"Drey, did you forget? Galoi are born without any sex characteristics." Tris stepped in to save him from his own stupidity.

"Oh yeah, sorry." Drey blinked and considered everything a long moment, rearranging his world view. "Anisoi Ureeya and his wife between them have seven *grown-up* children?"

Tris nodded. "Of course. They were both allowed to leave the home world, after all."

"And the *isoga* spouse, would she have had to *raise* three children also?"

"No. There is no *gamein* for *isoga*. There are too many already willing and eager to care for the few young that we have." The doctor answered that question. Really, she was remarkably forthcoming for a galoi. Well, for a galoi who wasn't Tris. Or maybe all galoi doctors were like this. Or maybe all galoi were like this in the safety of their own spaceship.

"So if they had all done their duty, why be sad about the victim being pregnant?"

The doctor looked upset herself at the question. Hard to tell with such stiff hair, but there was something in her big eyes – a true sadness. "Because we lost two lives instead of one."

# THE 10ᵀᴴ CHAPTER

## *Why aliens don't eat noodles*

They waited for nearly an hour, but Anisoi Ureeya and Belloi Froleb never returned.

Tris was happy enough because Drey kept touching him.

Drey also kept asking Belloi Rissib questions, but she became evasive, in that way that *isoga* get with younglings when they are too inquisitive about post-gender life.

Eventually Belloi Rissib outright instructed them to leave. They would be summoned to return when Anisoi Ureeya was ready to talk again.

Drey did not seem at all happy with this. Apparently, it was better to talk to possible suspects immediately, so as to "catch them unawares and emotional when they make more mistakes."

Tris thought this sounded a little cruel, but it was Drey's job to know things like that.

They left the spaceship and docking bay to be met *again* in the hallway by an overly enthusiastic Professor Frills. Tris usually admired enthusiasm but not this particular variety or in this particular man.

"Detective! I am eager to interview you once again. And Mr Zyga, perhaps you'll join us this time?"

"No," said Drey.

Tris was very impressed with Drey's firm tone and the

fact that he simply grabbed Tristol's hand and began tugging him bodily away from the academic.

Professor Frills scurried after them. "Oh, but detective, I must insist. Cultural debrief is mandated under station bylaws. You must officially reacclimatize to human existence after being aboard an alien vessel."

"We were there for less than an hour. That's ridiculous. No."

"Legally, you are required to—"

"So arrest me. Or would you like me to arrest myself? Since I don't think you have the authority or muscle to do it, Mr Anthropologist."

"Detective, now you're just being a jerk."

"Push me, professor. You've no idea how much of a jerk I can be." Drey stopped then, and swung so Tris was standing behind him.

Drey was guarding him from the professor. As Tris had guarded Drey twice that very day. Tris had fought against his *loga* nature to become protective, to make demands and assert dominance – things *loga* only ever did when they were in thrall to a *somate*. Tris had believed he would never get to know that part of himself, the part that wished to fight for the man he loved. Until Mr Joel had said those horrible things, teasing things as it turned out. *Perhaps I do not yet fully understand the human concept of teasing.*

And then he had done it again, when the *isoga* tried to claim Drey for sex and Drey had asked for his protection.

Twice in one day Tris had been *aggressive*. Him, Ooloi Tristol, once one of the sweetest, nicest *loga* ever to dance the orgies of choice, rolling about in the softest super-nests of the capital cities. There were some who would have sworn that Ooloi Tristol had not a single aggressive hormone in his hair. And yet. And yet, with Drey, he had felt anger. True anger.

And now Drey was posturing for him. In defense of him and his safety and well-being. Protecting him from a human. Admittedly the threat was a slimy pseudo-intellectual and probably not actually very dangerous. Drey himself being human, not galoi, it likely did not mean the same thing. But it was still thrilling.

The smaller human professor backed down so quickly it was basically a hair-flattening event.

Drey did not pause to savor his victory. He turned and put an arm about Tristol's waist and half lifted, half pushed him along, down the hallway at a rapid pace.

"We gotta go make a report to my boss. Then you gotta check in with your boss. If you want, you can relay through my ear-com. Then we need food."

"Yes, Drey, that is very kind of you. To share your com as well as share a meal with me again so soon, together. Did you bring me chopsticks?"

"Of course I did, baby."

Tristol's hair floated in pleasure. "Of course you did, Drey." *Somate.*

Drey realized they were already falling into a pattern of sorts and he loved it. Sure, neither of them had any kind of work schedule in place at the moment. They were at the whim of the investigation, which meant at the whim of the galoi. But still, he and Tris were developing couple's customs, like proper boyfriends, like a real relationship. Drey had wanted it for so long that he could hardly believe the reality of it, but he was determined to enjoy it.

Tristol's boss had entirely released him from his normal work schedule while he helped Drey with the investigation. Her voice, on the other end of Drey's ear-com, was amused.

"He forgot his coms again, didn't he?"

"Of course he did."

Drey was sitting across from Tris while his lover ate. They'd decided against noodles and gone for dorien food this time – ice cold *klepklep* in milky-fizzy *shmomu* blood, that warmed when it hit the mouth and reacted with the enzymes there in a truly alien fashion. Drey had learned to love it, but he knew a ton of humans who thought it way too weird. Apparently, Tris loved it, too.

Tristol's boss seemed to be rather a sweetheart. At least where Tris was concerned. Which Drey totally understood. Tris made him go all soft and gooey too. He'd never had much contact with the adjudicator except to bring a case before her, but he'd always respected her decisions and justice. He'd thought her quite tough. Apparently not so much with Tris.

"You feeding him, detective? He forgets to eat sometimes." She sounded almost, dare he think it, *mothering*.

"I am."

"You serious about him?"

"I am."

"If you hurt him, I'll space your ass so fast no one will even notice the vacuum breach."

"Understood, adjudicator."

"He doesn't have any family looking out for him."

"He's lucky to have you."

"Best attaché I've ever employed."

"He wants me to keep him."

"That's a good sign. He'll stay here on the station, then."

"So long as I stay here, I suppose."

"You the settling-down type, detective?"

"Yeah, and I like this station a lot."

"That's good, detective. That's real good."

"So?"

"So."

Drey smiled as Tristol's hair seemed to want to dip into his *klepklep*. Tris held it off with the hand not using chopsticks. Damn but he was beyond precious.

"I'll make sure you're on the guest list," insinuated Drey, coy.

"You do that."

Drey disconnected his com, grinning.

"Drey, are you throwing a human party gathering event?"

"*We're* throwing one, baby."

"We are? How wonderful. I have never thrown one before."

"After we solve this murder. And your people have boosted the hell out of here. And things have settled a bit. And you and I have lived together for a while. We'll revisit the kind of party I'm thinking about throwing."

"For which my boss will be a guest?"

"Yeah. She might even want to stand up with you. I think that'd be nice."

"Like dance together?"

"Not quite, baby."

"Good. She does not seem like the kind of female who dances."

Drey tried to imagine the fierce icy adjudicator bopping around at a club somewhere. He chuckled. "You're right. But the party I'm considering has a bit of a ritual to start it off. We'd be standing and reciting words for that."

"Oh, a religious human ritual? Are you religious, Drey? I never thought to ask."

"Not really. And this one is more cultural than religious."

"Oh, goody!" Tris almost clapped his hands in glee. His hair seemed to be trying to clap too. Drey wondered if Tristol's hair would start emoting like a human as Tris lived longer among them.

"I love human culture rituals. They are so very fascinating. I went to a natal day celebration once. There was open flame. Which was summarily extinguished. And cake. I like cake. It was fascinating *and* delicious."

"Someone blew out birthday candles?"

"Yes! I must say, however, that I have not particularly enjoyed human religious rituals so far. They tend to be somewhat boring. Except the janitors. They are fascinating." He lowered his voice. "But secret."

Drey decided it was cute that Tris apparently thought the station janitorial servicers were priests of some kind. "We'll make sure this particular ritual isn't boring."

"You will let me help plan it with you, Drey? How marvelous."

Drey grinned at him. He imagined Tris in one of his cute little suits, probably purchased special. Probably as close to his own lavender skin color as possible because that seemed to be important and very high on the desirability scale of clothing. Which meant Drey would have to wear a dark brown suit, to get as close as possible to his own skin tone. Because that's what Tris would want. And Drey was going to give his baby anything he wanted on their wedding day. He was already considering a piercing. A white stud, for his left ear.

Maybe he'd just go out and get one, surprise Tris with it. Or maybe that wasn't done. He'd better ask.

"Tris, baby?"

"Yes, Drey?"

"What would you say if I told you I wanted to have a stud earring put in this ear? Would that be okay with you?"

Suddenly he had a lap full of lavender and Tris was covering his face in *klepklep*-scented kisses, hair almost strangling him with its loving grip.

It was another full two shifts before they were asked back to the galoi ship. Apparently the *antiga* captain was finally prepared to be interviewed.

During that time, Drey filed his report and neatly dodged both Professor Frills and his boss's instructions to tender Professor Frills *all due professional courtesy*. He also went sock shopping with Tris, because Tris was very insistent about this.

Tris found him a number of charmingly patterned brown-tone socks. Drey hadn't the heart to tell him that human uniform custom dictated his socks match his pants, not his skin. But he figured no one really cared on this particular space station.

They ate together again, then went back to Tristol's quarters. Drey was beginning to forget what his own apartment looked like. He now found it weirdly arranged when he did stop by to change clothes.

Back at Tristol's place, Tris presented him with a fruit basket (for Drey's new socks) and placed it ceremonially in the exact middle of the empty bedroom where he kept all his suits.

Drey wrapped his arms around Tris from behind.

"Should we get another rack for the rest of my clothes, and move them in here too? Or would you prefer, while I'm here, that I just wander around all the time in nothing but the socks you picked out for me?"

Tris trembled. His hair was silken around Drey's neck and shoulders. "I think that is a very sexy idea, Drey, but I love even more the idea that you would move all your clothing in here with mine. I would take very good care of it. I would not let it get any holes at all."

So they went back to Drey's quarters and got all his clothes. And then – because Drey figured, why not? – they also collected his dishes and pots and pans, loading everything up into a little rep-tap hover-scoot for transport.

"We'll have to move some of the plants out of your kitchen, baby."

"They are only there because I did not realize a kitchen was for preparing food instead of growing it. Can we put the plants in the clothing room? Is that acceptable human interior arrangement?"

"Why not?"

"Hooray! I shall make that room so pretty. We will display the nicest of the clothes that we are not wearing."

"The ones that *you* are not wearing, baby. My clothes aren't very nice-looking."

"Oh, but they will be! Perhaps we can get some of those shelves humans are so fond of to display my shoes, too? I have never before owned so many pairs and I am very proud of them."

Drey, who only had three pairs himself (boots, loafers, and dress shoes he never wore) nodded sagely. He remembered he needed to get that one boot back from Joel. Loafers with his security uniform were not exactly regulation. Meanwhile, his baby could do whatever he wanted with their clothing. It sounded totally ridiculous to Drey, a room-sized closet full of plants and shoes, but he was about to go nest on the floor of a living room, so frankly, who the fuck cared?

"Could I set up a desk among all this vegetation and apparel?" He had this vision of an urban jungle, plants dangling from the ceiling, trailing leaves and flowers, interspersed with shirts, also hanging from the ceiling. And him sitting in a corner doing police work at a small desk, like something out of a really weird dream.

"Of course you can, Drey."

"It can be a pretty desk, but maybe sturdy enough for me to actually use, okay, Tris?"

"I have never owned any furniture before. A desk for you and shelves for my shoes. I am becoming so good at being human!"

"Not too good, okay, baby? I like you as a galoi."

At which said galoi became wrapped around him, coiled like his hair.

Drey chuckled and hoisted Tris up easily, hands on that perfect ass. Drey was amazed at how easily he'd gotten accustomed to Tristol's endless exuberance. He considered himself rather a reserved man, yet he was entirely comfortable with Tris.

He also appeared to have moved in with him, after only three days.

"This is fun, baby," he said gruffly, nuzzling Tristol's face with his beard.

"It is *perfect*." Tris trilled for him.

It was a while before they were summoned back to the galoi ship, but it really didn't seem like a long time to Drey.

"We're summoned to return. Should I wear the white suit, Tris?"

"Not yet."

"You ready, then?"

Tristol was wearing a very pale creamy brown suit this time. Drey thought it was probably something to do with him. Or with humans in general, since there was no purple to it at all. A statement of allegiance.

It looked beautiful on him.

*Drey is in my home.*

*Drey is staying.*

*Drey is keeping me.*

*I bought Drey socks!*

*Drey moved his clothes in with my plants.*

*Drey has pots and pans and cooking things in my kitchen.*

*I have a kitchen.*

*Drey can cook!*

*Drey may one day cook for me.*

*This is all so exciting.*

The litany repeated itself in Tristol's mind as they went back to the galoi spaceship to conduct, as Drey put it, *interrogations*. Which sounded so much more bad-ass than just interviews.

Tris liked the term *bad-ass*. It was a good term. He resolved to use it more often.

He did not think Drey was right. And he did not think Drey would get anything useful from his interrogations of Belloi Froleb and Anisoi Ureeya. But if Drey thought it was important, then Tris would support him.

This time it was Belloi Rissib who met them at the top of the ramp. Alone.

The *isoga* doctor led them to a common nest, a place where galoi ate and played and fucked. Tris supposed the setup would look peculiar to Drey. He would never have seen anything like it among humans. Humans did not seem to have such multi-use public areas, apart from hawker centers and parks. Codes of polite conduct were very particular in those places. No fucking. No sleeping.

"Is this a gym?" Drey asked, trying to connect the various shapes of the cushions and beds and blankets to something native to his own culture.

"Well, it is for *a kind of* exercise," hedged Tris, knowing humans were weird about what activities went where.

"Wait, this is an orgy room?"

"It is for sustenance and pleasure, in whatever form those take," explained Belloi Rissib.

Tris figured she was annoyed by Drey's confusion and his insistence on trying to put human names to something not at all human.

She went on. "We do everything together if possible, detective. Eat, sleep, sex. Only spousal groups are private. We all keep private quarters, as there are some who like to sleep alone and for the elimination of excrement, of course."

"No public restrooms, huh?" Drey looked approving. "Wait a second. That means when Tris said you have vids of the common areas, that means you have vids of *everything* taking place in those common areas?"

"Yes, detective."

"Isn't that, intrusive? Even the sex?"

"Detective, we are not weird and reclusive about coitus."

"But…"

"How do you know what your lover wants if you can not observe them in action? Humans are disgusting to hide their needs from each other as if such needs were somehow unhealthy."

"Okay, then." Drey went quiet, blinking, long-lashed and thoughtful. "Now I just feel really fucking weird about asking to see the vids. But I would still like to see them."

Belloi Rissib's hair twitched. "Would you indeed, detective? Why is that?"

"Because the victim had a full meal right before he was killed. And I'd like to see what happened to him during the course of that meal."

"How did you know that, detective?"

"I'm a detective. It's my business to detect."

"You are better than I expected. Very well. I will mention this to our tech and get you the vid that you require." The doctor inclined her head.

Tris admired the control she had over her hair. He wondered how old she was. Did it come from experience or a certain coldness of heart?

"You will have to watch it here, detective. You can not leave our ship with the vid data."

"I figured. You don't have to ask the captain first?"

She said, "I do not think Anisoi Ureeya will object. But I am permitted to make this decision without him. His wish is to prevent galoi contamination by alien thought. He will not care if you are contaminated by us and our culture, detective."

Tris thought Drey would have objected to that, except his big human suddenly paused and grinned and looked over at him. "I think I'm pretty contaminated already. I love Tristol's nest."

Belloi Rissib made the comfort-rumble of *isoga*

amusement at the antics of a youngling. "Of course you do. He is so pretty, your *zyga*. I bet he makes a beautiful nest."

Tristol preened and he couldn't stop his hair from puffing up in pleasure. To be noticed at all was flattering, but to be complimented as a *zyga* was unheard of. He was beginning to like Belloi Rissib.

Still, he would not insult her by verbally acknowledging her praise. His fluffy hair was enough.

"This room is intriguing." Drey's eyes were focused and interested as he took in the large common-nest around them.

"To us it is normal."

To Tris it was achingly familiar but somehow not upsetting.

He realized that he now preferred his hawker center with the noodles made however he wished. Galoi did not have noodles. Too much like hair, probably. Tris also preferred the short green grass of the park where the dirty human young played and shrieked. And he preferred to go home with Drey and ride that big purple penis in his own nest like a fully matured and mated *loga* rather than play in the common nests of his youth. That was a pleasure he had thought he would never get. It was worth giving this up for.

*Somate* had been the only thing about Gal that Tris truly regretted leaving behind. But since, when he took *zyga*, *somate* had merely been a wish and not a reality, and he had already lived many years without one, Tris had figured it did not really matter. Now Drey had made it matter more than anything. So Tris would take the human space station with all its oddness – his neighbors asking him to fix things and noodles like chewy hair and Drey – over the familiar comforts of his home world. And he would be glad for what he had. So *very* glad.

Eventually, Belloi Froleb and Anisoi Ureeya joined them.

Belloi Rissib stayed while Drey conducted his interrogation, which did not surprise Tris (*isoga* were protective *and* nosy) but caused Drey to arch both brows in human confusion and interest.

Drey suggested they all five sit on an *ootill* pouffe. A nice big one with lots of room to take on different positions, and little straps to hold the *logas* down. Because most *logas* enjoyed that and hair was not always reliable in the matter of restraint.

Tris carefully did not tell Drey what an *ootill* pouffe was *actually* used for because he thought Drey might get embarrassed. And, frankly, it did materially deflate the gravity of the word *interrogation*, if that *interrogation* was conducted atop a massive sex cushion.

Drey asked a number of questions concerning how Belloi Froleb felt about Anisoi Ureeya fucking the dead *loga*. (Before he was dead, of course, because otherwise – yecch!) He asked how she felt about Ooloi Villisol becoming pregnant.

The *isoga* answered all questions simply and with no hair-movement under her veil. As expected, she was a little sad, her voice gruff and her eyes heavy-lidded.

Then Drey turned his attention onto Anisoi Ureeya and basically the same thing happened. Although he did keep asking the *antiga* if he knew how the *loga* came to skip his birth control pills.

Anisoi Ureeya was obviously annoyed but kept repeating that he had no idea and that he assumed it must be a mistake.

Drey was clearly getting frustrated. This was not what he had expected.

Tris was not surprised at all.

Drey wanted to interrogate their other spouse, Ooloi Marrel. But Belloi Froleb refused. As she should. She was an *isoga* guarding her *somate*. Besides, the result of any conversation with the *loga* would be just as useless, Tris had no doubt.

Drey was looking for human motive but there was none to uncover.

They were at an impasse.

Drey asked, possibly of Tris but clearly willing to take anyone's answer. "Is it obvious when a *loga* is in heat? Like physically or emotionally or in the hair or anything?"

Anisoi Ureeya answered him. "No, detective. Is it obvious with your human birth givers?"

"Sometimes. My sister used to get really fucking crabby. And hungry. And oddly clumsy."

"Mood modulation? No." Belloi Rissib jumped in using her doctor training. "Sometimes there is a minor elevation in temperature, but we have been unable to predict estrus based on this."

Drey nodded. "Yet another reason your people have trouble conceiving?"

Belloi Rissib did not answer that. "There is a way to surgically know, of course, but the act of checking would stop the estrus so why bother?"

"Why have a birth control pill at all? You'd think you'd want pregnancy as much as possible."

"Because *gamein* is hard enough on a *loga's* body, detective. We are aliens, not monsters. Once the commitment has been satisfied, duty completed, we place no more restrictions on either *loga* or *antiga*. There are sperm suppressants available, as well."

"You are not taking those, captain?"

"No." A short answer. Anisoi Ureeya was not the type to suppress. Tris recognized an *antiga* who was proud of his virility.

Drey rubbed his beard, clearly planning his next words carefully. "Fine, captain."

Tris winced. He wished Drey would use the correct title. Humans always defaulted to titles of function, galoi always used titles of identity. It mattered not that Anisoi Ureeya was the captain of this spaceship, but it was vital that he was *antiga*. So *anisoi* should *always* be used.

But Drey was too human to even realize his breach of

etiquette. He pressed on. "Captain, you have this *mycota* but you don't have a *male loga* as part of your spousal group. Yet you have a stated sexual preference for that, as well as all the others." He gestured at Anisoi Ureeya's preference ear with its four rings on proud display. "Do you also have a sexual *compulsion* to seek coitus with a *male loga* outside of your *mycota*? Forgive me if I didn't phrase that properly."

"Forgiven and no."

"Would other galoi?"

"No."

Tristol tried to explain. "Drey, did I tell you that I met a human bisexual once? He was married to a gay human male but did not seem to find it necessary to seek out women. Although he liked them as much as men, he said. It is like that."

Drey nodded his acknowledgment.

Everyone else in the room, of course, ignored Tris.

Drey sighed. "Well, then, thank you for your time, Anisoi. Belloi." He turned to Belloi Rissib. "You said you would get me the vid-feed of Ooloi Villisol's meal in the common area directly prior to his death?"

She nodded. "I have a wall prepared for your use, just over there." She gestured to another part of the room, where a nest was arranged for viewing in front of a multi-function entertainment wall.

She walked over and lay down.

"Drey, you should go lie next to her."

"I should?"

"Yes, Drey."

Drey did so, looking very uncomfortable. Although Tris was certain the nest was quite soft and perfectly arranged. Drey was not so very big he could not fit, although his feet did dangle off the end. His uniform pants rose up and showed off his socks. *Nice socks. Mine.*

The nest auto-adjusted itself and angled perfectly to see

the screen. Tris crouched behind Drey and craned his neck to see, too. It was not comfortable but it was better than joining them, which felt wrong. Too reminiscent of his pre-*zyga* days. Tris did not want to think of Drey as belonging to that time – a time when Tris did not know who he was and was not comfortable with his own identity.

# THE 11ᵀᴴ CHAPTER

## *Favorite shade of purple*

The vid was a goddam revelation.

The segment Drey was permitted to watch started with the room already full, a dozen or so galoi eating and socializing. Fortunately none of them were fucking – at least not on screen.

The room itself looked very like the one they were in at the moment, slightly different colors, but just as comfortable and attractive and odd. Drey hesitated to call it a mess hall. He suspected the galoi present in the vid represented about a quarter of the full ship's complement. Galoi likely had some kind of shift rotation in place – otherwise, there were way fewer of them aboard than he had guessed from the size of the spaceship.

The galoi in the vid gathered in groups and curled up together in apparently arbitrary numbers and configurations. They mostly hung out in one big commercial nest-bed-thingy, where they drank their food out of bowls. A few podded off onto smaller nests or large cushions, slightly separate for a while, but then would inevitably come back to the larger group. They seemed to be almost always pressed against each other or touching one another. They were tactile creatures, always petting, hair entwining – the line between friend and lover and intimate was not just blurred, it was nonexistent.

To Drey's human eyes it looked alien and odd, but also warm and loving. It was hard to tell from the vid's angle who was whom. But he assumed, because of all he'd learned so far, that most of the crew were *isoga*. The purples tended to be middle shades and have pink overtones. They were also mostly bigger than Tris. Drey felt, given what he'd learned about breeding issues, that he was safe in guessing *isoga*.

At one point two lighter purple bodies came onto the screen. These were given lots of care and attention. *Loga*, Drey suspected. They never seemed to have to get up or do anything – some *isoga* or another would rush away and reappear, offering a bowl or a cup or a toy. Nearby *isoga* always made certain the *loga* was settled comfortably in the nest.

No wonder Tris was always so pleased when Drey took care of him.

"Tris, will you please explain what's happening?"

The doctor, lying next to Drey and far too close, was watching Drey rather than the vid, and seemed no longer inclined to talk. He could feel her cool breath on his cheek and it made him shiver, not in a good way.

Tris, who was crouched behind him, tucked his head over Drey's shoulder on the opposite side. It was done with such easy affection it made Drey happy, but he now realized, this was also something totally natural to all galoi. No wonder Tris constantly wanted to pet him and climb into his lap, wrap himself around Drey's body. Tris not only liked to touch, he *needed* to be touched. Drey resolved to make certain he was always holding his baby's hand, at the very least, when they were out and about. He didn't mind at all – in fact, he enjoyed the idea. There was a claiming to it which Tris would not understand, but would make Drey proud and warn other men away.

Tris began to whisper to Drey, explaining a little of what was happening on the vid, often using galoi words because galactic standard was insufficient. He pointed out lovers and friends and possibly both. He distinguished spousal groups. There were *isoga mycota* pairs, since there was no restriction on *isoga* marrying each other. Two of these also included one each of the *loga*.

Drey found himself quickly looking at the ears of any new galoi entering the room. There were many who had no studs, but all had rings in their right ear and usually at least two different colors. Drey got very good at recognizing preferences.

He did eventually see, in the upper corner of one part of the screen, two *isoga* getting each other off. Which was hot, and totally not something one expected at the dinner table – or in the dinner nest. But which didn't seem to upset any of the other galoi present.

Finally, the petite mauve form of Ooloi Villisol appeared.

His hair was neutral, although arranged very oddly, hanging forward and around his face. He was treated much as the other *loga* before him. As soon as he was noticed, one of the *isoga* bought him a bowl of food and ushered him to the largest nest. But when the *isoga* would have cuddled next to him, stroked his hair while he ate, Ooloi Villisol rebuffed her.

"He's eating alone." Drey pointed out the obvious.

Tristol's voice was high with no trill to it at all. "That is not normal. His hair, too. We do not do that style."

They kept watching as the young galoi accepted a drink, again rebuffing the *isoga* who brought it to him.

"Why does he not want contact?" Tristol asked, as if Drey might have the answers.

"Is he unwell? Do galoi get sick?" Drey tried.

"Like with virus or bacteria or genetic disorders? Certainly not as much as humans. Galoi are very resilient. But we need to be. We cannot so easily replace population lost to war or disease or stupidity."

"You don't wage war to conquer?" Drey wanted confirmation of this.

"Oh no, we have no soldiers, only *isoga* fight and they are protectors, guards. They will defend Gal and our young to their last breath, but there is no reason to actively hunt other sentient creatures and certainly not other galoi. We have no need to expand or to colonize. Remember, Drey, we do not have the numbers necessary to do so."

Drey nodded, still intent on watching the vid. The victim was eating, but Drey couldn't tell if anything like the big trumpet flower was going into his mouth. Plus Joel had specified, *after* the meal.

After.

"So why leave Gal to work on experimental tech in a spaceship, then?"

"Intellectual advancement is always encouraged, Drey. Just because we do not kill does not mean we cannot evolve."

Drey snorted. "Point taken. He's moving."

The victim stood. An *isoga* appeared to take away his empty bowl and cup. They exchanged a few words. Then the boy, still alone, moved to leave the common area.

"He has isolated himself," said Tris, sounding very sad.

"I take it that's a bad sign."

"For *loga* in particular."

"Yeah, baby, I figured you were a social little thing. Always befriending everyone. Come by your gregariousness naturally, do you?"

"Yes, Drey."

"Wait!" *What the hell was that?* Drey turned to the *isoga* doctor lying too close in the nest next to him. Which, after what he'd just learned could occur in a room like this one, had a whole new layer of meaning. Especially given the black ring in her ear and the glint in her eye.

"Rewind it, please."

She made a sharp clicking noise and the vid rewound.

"Stop!"

She stopped it and it resumed normal play.

"Pause!"

Another click and the vid froze.

"Can you increase the magnification on his head?"

"Why?"

"Please, Belloi Rissib!"

The vid shifted and magnified while she made a complex series of clicking noises.

Drey pointed. "His hair moved a bit. See? There, his right ear is party exposed."

Tristol, behind him, made a pathetic keening warble.

Drey gave voice to his realization while looking hard at the doctor. "He isn't wearing any earrings. He took them out. Or had them stolen."

Her face was difficult to read, even as close as she was. And her hair was still stiff. But he thought she was sad. Really, very sad. And maybe a little sick. Yet Tris had just said that galoi didn't get sick.

Drey struggled to sit up and extract himself from the weird massive cushion.

Tristol's little chin was no longer pressed against his shoulder.

Turns out that was because Tris was curled in a ball on the floor, whimpering.

Drey sat down right there and gathered him up into his lap, cradled him close, and turned to look at Belloi Rissib, who was still lying motionless staring at the image on the vid.

"The dead body had earrings."

"Yes, it did," answered the doctor. "I remember. He must have changed his mind and put them back in before he died."

"Changed his mind? Changed his mind about what?"

The doctor, still staring at the screen, said something in galoi.

Tristol reared back and spat something lyrical back at

her. But she'd clearly decided that today she was ignoring the *zyga*.

"What just happened, Tris, what did you say?"

"She said she could not believe it of him. She said it was not acceptable. She said he was too smart, too brilliant. Remember, he was on board without *gamein* because he was an engineering genius of some kind?"

"I remember, Tris, of course I do."

"Oh, yes. You said you thought that was a reason for him to die. But now his ears are naked."

"And what exactly does that mean in this instance?"

"He intended *zyga*." Tristol's voice shook. "He intended *zyga* and someone stopped him. And he was pregnant, Drey! He was pregnant but he wanted out. Nothing could be worse."

Tristol's miserable shuddering subsided. He went stiff in Drey's arms. His hair kinked.

*Uh oh.*

"Anisoi Ureeya *trapped* him!"

Drey frowned. His brain hurt. Crime and aliens combined to make the threads more difficult to trace than usual. Or should he say hairs? He knew he was still missing something. "By getting him pregnant? Yes, but the captain probably wouldn't want to kill him."

"It is the same thing!" cried Tris.

"No, actually, it isn't, baby. Fuck, this is a mess."

The doctor was still not speaking.

Drey sighed. "Belloi Rissib, I'll need to watch the vids for every meal Ooloi Villisol attended, going back at least two galactic weeks, or whatever the equivalent is in galoi. We need to see when he stopped putting his earrings in, and what might have triggered such a major change."

"I will need time to get those for you, detective. Two galactic hours, please."

Drey thought that was a good thing. It would give him time to get Tris calmed down.

Tristol let Drey guide him off the galoi spaceship, keeping in physical contact, holding his hand. This was a thing humans did with their young and their lovers. It was a little like twining hair strands and almost as comforting. Drey even threaded their fingers together, like true intimates.

Tristol took reassurance from that.

They moved quickly through the docking bay and out into the hallway of the station.

Drey did not look at or speak to Professor Frills, who was, as expected, waiting for them just outside the door.

The professor, eager and undaunted, followed them all the way back to Zone 3, at which juncture Drey took a few quick swerves through the hawker center and then ducked behind Mistress Zing's ramen stall. Xe winked at them as they dodged into xer *personal*cooking*private*noodle-preparation* area, which Tris had thought was *utterly sacred and off limits*.

They stayed there for a few minutes while Mistress Zing sent Professor Frills off with a bowl of ramen that he did not want and a few well-chosen words that he also did not want. Both would do him good – Professor Frills was skinny and rude.

Xe stuck xer head into the back area to say the extremely oddly phrased, "Coast is clear, sweet cheeks." *What did coastal waterways have to do with anything? And why were Drey's cheeks sweet? If anything, they were salty. Especially when he was aroused.*

"Thanks, hot stuff," replied Drey.

Which made much better sense because Mistress Zing did in fact serve *hot stuff* at xer noodle stall.

"I thought I was the main recipient of your endearments, Drey," huffed Tris, worried.

"I save the best ones for you."

"You do? *Honey* and *baby* are the best ones?"

"Yeah, baby."

"Very well, then. I accept your endearment ranking system."

Drey had yet to let go of his hand and was now using it to tug Tris around the very back of the stall, into a part of the station Tristol did not know.

This was the secret area where the people who did useful things that kept the station running were located. These were the impressive humans who fixed, and tidied, and made the station functional and beautiful – the ritual janitor clergy that everyone pretended not to see (like *zyga*) but who were glorious in their blue uniforms and serious expressions. Tristol always spoke in hushed tones around these humans. They controlled the cleaning robots, and the air flow, and the gravity matrix, and, most importantly, the wall colors and the lighting. They were vital and to be revered. Although, to be honest, he had not yet determined if they also *actually* served a religious function.

Tris was very nervous about being in their sacred space.

They seemed to know Drey, however, and did not object to him being there. So Tris stuck close to his *somate*.

Drey knew his way around, too. He guided Tris through the chaos. Perhaps Drey was a pilgrim or prophet, to traverse so easily between social spaces.

Tris kept his eyes lowered and his hair controlled out of respect.

Soon they popped out of a door and into a hallway familiar to Tris.

"We are near my quarters!"

"Yes, baby. I figured you'd like the comfort of home around you right now."

"Please, Drey."

Drey unsealed the door.

Tris had been quick to enable Drey's ID for his door. He hated remembering to seal the thing and Drey cared about security. Obviously.

Immediately inside, Drey kicked off his loafers and then bent to pull off Tristol's shoes. Then he guided Tris into the wonderful familiarity of his own beloved nest.

There Drey held him close.

Tris lay perfectly still and let himself feel safe. His mind spun out with possibilities. He could not stop imagining what it would feel like to be impregnated against his will, before he could escape Gal. It was the most horrifying idea. Inconceivable, really. There were so many safety measures in place, inculcated into galoi culture, to prevent it from happening. He knew he had not the words in galactic to help Drey understand any of it.

Perhaps, just perhaps, the earrings had been *taken* from Ooloi Villisol? Perhaps there was a mistake in his nakedness. Perhaps he had not wanted *zyga*? That would be so much better to think on than any other option. So Tris chose to believe that, and ignore the horror rippling through his hair.

"Can I ask a question not to do with the case, baby?"

"Oh please, Drey. I should like to be distracted. My thoughts are not pleasant."

"I'm not sure this will help, but still, I'm kinda curious. You need to be penetrated to climax. I'm assuming it's the same with all *loga* and has to do with the *antiga* and his barbed cock."

This was exactly the kind of distraction Tris needed. To talk of sex was almost as much fun as to have sex.

Also, Drey was so adorably awkward whenever he tried to wade through the nuances of galoi coitus. Tris only just kept his hair from shaking in amusement at Drey's funny, awkward facial expression. He didn't want Drey to feel mocked for his ignorance. Humans were so very good at fucking, so desperate to engage in it, and yet so uncomfortable talking about it.

"Yes, Drey. I need the *antiga's* barb, or as we have discovered, a really large pretty purple human dick pounding into me and against my—"

Drey cleared his thought. "Yes, baby, I get that part."

Drey's penis got it too. Apparently it enjoyed this kind of discussion more than Drey's face did.

Tris decided that sex would be an even better distraction from the horrors of the last few hours, so he reached down to squeeze and touch. He used more force than he would with a galoi lover.

Drey groaned. "Later, baby. Let me ask this before I lose my courage."

Tris sighed and stopped playing. His hair, however, kept stroking where ever it wished.

"So if *loga* need this specific thing to climax, why would any *loga* wear an *isoga* earring?"

Tristol's hair actually did shake at that. *Funny question!* "Well, there are always toys, and hands, and other innovative options. We are not prudes or anything. Besides, not everyone is as obsessed with sex only for the sake of orgasm as you humans." He grinned. "And me, of course. I am rather selfish. Hence the one earring only. There are even some *loga* who wear the copper earring."

"For *female isoga*?"

"Yes. It is considered a little perverted but not off limits. And of course, she would only have toys and appendages to fuck her *loga* with. But I guess such a *loga* also wants breasts and such." Tristol made a face of human disgust to get his point across.

Drey laughed at him. "Takes all sorts to make a world?"

"Yes, Drey. Or, as another human adage says – *there is no accounting for taste*. Although, of course, we galoi do account for it. We make lists and categories and wear jewelry and other indicators. So really, for galoi there is *only* accounting for taste. It is very important that taste *be* accounted for, so that everyone can be happy, and have sex with everyone else that they want to."

"Sounds exhausting," said Drey.

"Yes, that too. Sex is good recreational entertainment *and* exercise. Especially in groups."

"Do you miss it?"

Tris thought about the vid that they had watched. "I miss touch most of all. I miss *isoga* care on occasion. I miss the *knowing* that comes with community but mostly, no, I do not miss it. With you and this here and what we are becoming together, I do not miss it at all. I get so much now."

He petted up Drey's chest under his shirt. When Drey did not stop him like earlier, Tris pulled the shirt off of his lover.

Drey's skin was so warm and dark, his nipples were so fascinating and sensitive. He stroked them with his hair while his hands explored lower.

This time Drey let him squeeze.

"What do you get instead, Tris?"

"New things. Things no other galoi will know. This space station is unique to me, no other galoi will come here. No other *zyga*. We are each exiles on our own journeys, learning new things about other races – about stars and planets and space stations and ramen." He bent and nuzzled Drey's chest, petting all of his human's lovely muscles with hair and hands.

"I have learned how to maintain a cat, Drey. No other galoi has ever done such a thing. I have eaten noodles cooked by an alien born of two species. I have seen a leader with fragmented eyes and a warrior with painted skin. I have tasted *klepklep*. And I have learned about honeymoons, although I do not yet completely understand them."

Drey chuckled under him, and lifted up his hips so Tris could strip him of the bottom part of his uniform.

"That's a lot of things to have learned, baby." Drey was now wearing a pair of his new socks and nothing else.

Tris left the socks on, admiring how pretty they were

against Drey's skin. *I did that. I made this moment beautiful.*

Then he stroked up to Drey's penis. It was hard, but not as swollen as it could get, when it turned from brown to dark violet, a color Tris had now decided was his very favorite in all the universe. Because it was as if Drey's penis knew that Tris was galoi. Knew that it was about to fuck lavender. Knew that its place was there inside Tris.

Tris trilled at that thought, and bent to lick, hoping to get it really hard, to achieve that ideal purple hue. He lapped and fondled and his hair played too.

Drey gasped. "Do that again!"

Tris obliged, sucking the head of Drey's penis into his mouth. Mouthing over it, careful of sharp teeth, swirling with his tongue. When it popped back out, it was gloriously purple – galoi-colored.

Tris wondered if he could find a pair of socks in that color.

He looked up at his lover, prepared to continue their conversation.

Drey was panting and his eyes were closed. He was so gorgeous.

"And that, Drey, is what I have explored in just the last few months aboard this station. On Gal I would have had only one life. Among the stars I get to live many."

"And now you're sharing mine?"

"Yes, Drey. And you will teach me so much. You have already said I will understand honeymoons. After the first one, will you take me on a *second* one? I understand each is different and the second has to do with umbrellas."

Drey chuckled but also moved, flipping and arranging Tris so that he was on his knees and forearms, so Drey could drive into him.

Tris was delighted by this. He loved all the positions that got Drey's penis into his ass, but this one gave Drey the best leverage so he could pound really hard.

"As many honeymoons as possible, baby, so long as we do them together." Drey reached around to gather up Tristol's cum, slicked himself, and then pushed in – a smooth, solid slide until he hit Tris deep and exactly right.

Tris had no words any more. He forgot galactic standard. He forgot galoi. He was nothing but quivering trills and vibrant hair – filled and loved.

Drey was inside him, purple with his need, and Tris was all his, lavender with his acceptance. Lavender with happiness.

Afterward, Drey had lifted Tristol, taken him into the cleansing unit to freshen them both, murmuring words of love and praise the entire time. Then he took him back to the hawkers to feed him and loan him chopsticks.

Tris tried to stop himself from thinking, over and over, about the dead *loga*.

*Poor Ooloi Villisol.* All Drey's good work in their nest and Tristol's hair was stiffening and his heart was hurting again.

When they got back to their nest, Tris suggested that Drey change into the white suit.

So Drey did. It was stark and almost painfully bright against his skin.

They returned to the galoi spaceship. Tris felt he had armed his *somate* the best he could, weaponized him with contrast.

Belloi Froleb met them this time at the top of the ramp – alone and veiled. She did not see Tris. Which was as it should be.

She led them back to the same nesting area as before. There he and Drey spent hours going over vids.

Belloi Froleb ran the feed silently at Drey's request. She totally ignored Tris, although he cuddled next to Drey on the viewing cushion this time. He needed the warmth and the roughness of Drey's beard as a reminder of humanness – safety and home.

Tris kept himself together and tried as best he could to help Drey understand what they were watching.

In the beginning vids, Ooloi Villisol was wearing his two earrings and interfacing happily. He was flirting and caressing and engaging with his fellow shipmates. He seemed excited and pleased to be on a spaceship at all, which Tris could understand. The life of a *loga* was a sheltered one, before *gamein.*

Tris had been pretty good at sneaking away and going out where he should not. He had also had contact-training early, so even before he was summoned to *gamein,* he had traveled to other lands on Gal. But few *loga* were so proactive in pursuit of freedom at such a young age. Tris supposed he should have known himself from the beginning. That he was secretly *zyga.*

When Tris had been summoned to complete himself, when they started to push *antiga* candidates at him, he had turned them all down. They would hunt for another genetic match. Tris would turn him down too. This went on for years. Decades. Ooloi Tristol refusing *gamein* by rejecting perfectly decent *antiga* until – until the end when Tris realized why. He had acknowledged the truth to himself, curled in a ball of misery in a nest that had never felt right, where his paint strokes were tentative and miserable. His home, his home world, was alien to him. So he had made all the necessary arrangements and chosen his advocate of record. He had stood proud when he made his petition, and told his truth, and was exiled forever.

Ooloi Villisol in the vid was a pretty, vibrant, mauve young man, happy, bouncy. Then as the time lapse progressed, as they moved in the vids from one day to the next, closer to his murder, he faded. He lost not only his vibrancy of color but his innate exuberance for life. He was struggling with something that wilted his hair and body.

The *isoga* hurried to him – tending to him, trying to cheer him up as best they knew how. But they did not understand what was going on either.

Then came the vid where Anisoi Ureeya approached Ooloi Villisol for sex. They left the common nest together. Tristol explained to Drey that it looked arranged. Like someone had gone to the captain, hoping the one *antiga* aboard might be the thing this *loga* needed to pull him back from colorlessness.

Only it obviously made everything worse.

At one point, Drey said, unprompted, "His earrings! They aren't in the same order."

"What?" Tris was confused.

Drey explained. "The gold one is on top, the black one underneath. When I examined that boy's body, the black one was on the top. They've been switched."

"Then someone else put them back in him," said Tris with confidence. "Probably after he died."

Belloi Froleb seemed to be trying not to pay attention to their conversation. She was lying near them to watch and control the vid, but a full arm's length away from Drey, who had Tris curled against him as they discussed what the vid feeds showed, spooling out above them.

Tris explained to his human lover. "The order of the rings is at the whim of the wearer, but once settled, it never changes. Someone knew Ooloi Villisol wore two but did not pay close enough attention to put them back in correctly."

Drey nodded.

They continued watching.

Tris reached up and petted Drey's rough beard for comfort. There was something about the alien nature of the hair on his human's face that was reassuring. Watching the galoi world play out before him was so achingly familiar, yet so very, very wrong.

Ooloi Villisol continued to withdraw from his

shipmates, even after fucking Anisoi Ureeya, until at long last came the vid that they had seen already.

Ooloi Villisol walked into the common nest with no earrings at all.

Tris shuddered all over again at the courage of it. To go bare into a common nest. To show everyone his choice and his shame. To make such a statement so loudly for all to see. A statement that could never be taken back.

And yet.

And yet. He had kept his ears covered with his hair. He had not really been that bare. But he had still done it. He had walked among the galoi a grown man with naked ears.

Hidden. But naked.

"A *loga* only removes earrings for one reason." Tris swallowed, searching for galactic among the music of his galoi words. "Drey, you must find out if he filed any official documentation with the home world."

Drey turned to Belloi Froleb. "Did he?"

"Did he what?"

"Did he file any documentation?" Drey cuddled Tris close and then asked the right question, because he was smart and he learned and he was a good detective. "Did he request *zyga* state?"

"Do not use that word, human!"

"Ask if he *requested advocacy*," whispered Tris.

"Did he request advocacy?" Drey asked the *isoga*, obediently.

Her voice was cool and calm. "I do not know."

"Could you find out, please?"

"He would need to go through a medical professional for that request," Tris explained.

"He would?"

"Yes, as I did."

The *isoga* stood, abrupt and formal. "I will go find Belloi Rissib."

Drey and Tris were left briefly alone in the big room,

still lying in front of the vid as it continued to play out scenes of galoi intimacy that Tristol no longer needed.

"Tris, is it possible our victim put the earrings back in because he found out he was pregnant? Would that change his mind, do you think? Stop him from *zyga*?"

Tris seriously considered this, tried hard to separate his own complex emotions about *zyga* state. It was not possible. "I can only speak for myself. But no. I would have felt violated, not happy, to be carrying young. Every fiber of my being would be against it, would want to escape."

Tris shuddered with all his hair and his body. "It is a horrible thought, to be in such a situation. It is why *loga* are given time to take *gamein*. We are given a choice of *antiga* to fuck for our three births, within reason and using the government's genetic matching system, of course. We are coaxed into our duties, pampered. *Loga* should not and cannot be forced. *Zyga* is taken only out of absolute necessity and never from spite. It is the worst possible choice for any galoi to make, let alone a *loga*." He gestured to the vid where his people touched and fucked and loved each other. "You see how we are, Drey? You have insight now into the galoi. Insight no other human possesses. We are together. We are *always* together. We are cared for and connected. A galoi in exile is in pain, for we have lost everything. We *zyga* leave because we *must*, not because we will."

# THE 12TH CHAPTER

## *But we don't have a word for that, either!*

There was a shift and lyrical murmuring behind them.

Drey turned to see.

Bellois Froleb and Rissib had returned.

Anisoi Ureeya was with them.

The three galoi moved closer as a unit. Belloi Froleb's hand was resting on the captain's back. His dark purple hair was curled down and around her supportive arm. Her face was utterly impassive. His looked interested and a little sad. The doctor's hair was perfectly still as she exerted control over it. It looked painful. They were all three watching Drey, but they would listen to Tris. Drey would make them if he had to.

Drey glared at them all – frustrated that he had just watched a beautiful mauve man crumble into misery while they, his own people, did nothing to save him. "Did you see what was happening to him?"

Anisoi Ureeya's hair was limp. Obviously unhappy because he had slept with the victim.

Drey accused him of that, lashing out, unprofessional. "You fucked him in order to try and fix him."

It was not a question but the captain took it as such. "Yes, detective. It did not work."

"Obviously. Tristol assures me it would've made things worse."

The captain's hair wilted even more. He was genuinely gutted about that. His *isoga* spouse made a protective, rumbling growl noise at Drey.

Drey ignored her.

The captain's sadness seemed to hurt Tris too, because he spoke to the *antiga*, even though the other galoi still refused to acknowledge his existence. "The act of sex itself did not hurt him, *anisoi*, just the results. Pregnancy would have made everything horrible for Ooloi Villisol."

The doctor, the only one so far to acknowledge Tris to his face, rumbled out the question, "Why?"

There was a lot of emotion behind that word – defense, accusation, fear. All feelings Drey had dealt with before. Feelings he understood, whatever the species. *Guilt.*

Drey extracted himself from the viewing nest, leaving the vid running behind him. He helped Tris to his feet, and pulled him so they were standing and facing the galoi. He and Tris, together, against a whole alien race.

He glared at the doctor. "You're the one who fucked with his heat suppressants."

The *isoga's* hair stayed flat.

Tristol keened. "Why? Why would you do that, Belloi Rissib?"

"I knew he was having doubts. He asked me for advocacy." The doctor's hair wilted and then stiffened. Drey wondered if that was the galoi version of a shrug.

Tristol clutched at Drey's hand and leaned heavily against his side. He was horrified. "And you denied him? And then you set him up to go into heat and arranged for sex with Anisoi Ureeya, with an *antiga*?"

The doctor did not look at all repentant. "Of course I did. *Loga* are meant to be pregnant. Once properly inseminated, he would understand his place, remember who he was and who he was meant to be. He would see how easy it is, and then he could go home, birth his three, and remain a productive galoi. Remain with us."

Tristol seemed barely able to stand. He was shaking now against Drey. His hair and his body both vibrated.

Drey looked down at him, wondering how he could help.

Tristol's hair was moving between wilted and spiked into kinks – sorrow and anger in equal measure.

Tris spoke to all the galoi in front of him. He clearly no longer cared if they pretended to hear him or not. The doctor heard. She had always acknowledged Tristol's existence. Drey had actually liked her a little, once, because of that.

Drey was proud of the strength in Tristol's voice. "Ooloi Villisol found out he was pregnant and realized he was trapped. Should his young be viable, Gal would never let him go." Tris angled to look up at Drey. "A *loga* must choose exile *before gamein*. There is a galoi saying – the mind can only be open if the womb is forever closed."

Drey wrinkled his nose. "So *zyga* is some sort of weird quasi-virgin sacrifice thing?"

Tris only blinked at him.

Drey was a detective, so he kept everyone focused. "Who killed him under these circumstances? It still doesn't make sense. Everyone has every reason for wanting him to stay alive. The whole species has reason."

"I do not know, Drey."

Drey puffed out his breath and tried for a different approach. "How would you have felt, Tris, if you were put into this situation? You're the only one here who can give us any insight."

"Oh, I—" Tristol paused. Then he whined out a long string of galoi. It was the first time Drey heard the language not sound musical. He suspected these were curse words.

Then Tristol moved, jumped, plastered himself against Drey – chest-to-chest, trying to climb up him. Almost as if he were trying to climb *inside* him – desperate for comfort. His hair was so limp it was almost dead-looking and flat. He was whimpering in distress.

"Okay, baby, okay." Drey scooped him up and held him close, rubbing his back, petting his hair, one hand under his ass to keep him stabilized. He stared over his shoulder to the shocked faces of the three galoi opposite him.

Both the captain and the doctor had moved forward slightly, their hair stretching out, instinctively wanting to comfort a distressed *loga*. Even Belloi Froleb's icy regard was cracking under Tristol's obvious pain.

Tris kept up his keening, tight against Drey, until finally he gulped and calmed. He turned his head and glared, mostly at the doctor. He spat out a string of beautiful lyrical words that caused the three other galoi to start speaking at once. Purple hair of various shades waved all over the place (what was not veiled) and purple arms gesticulated. It was like watching very aggravated bipedal sea anemones.

Drey didn't speak galoi, but he knew denial when he saw it.

"Tris? Baby?"

"He did it to *himself*, Drey." Tristol remembered his galactic standard at last, choked out the words. "He picked the flower and he ate it *himself*."

"Suicide?"

"We do not have a word for that, either. As uncommon as murder is for galoi, suicide cannot be comprehended."

"Then Tris, how can you know this about him?" Drey had to be certain.

"Of course I know this." Tristol shifted, impatient, vibrating with energy now instead of grief.

Drey set him back down.

His lover began to move, back and forth in the small space between where Drey stood and where the other three galoi faced him.

Tris paced but he wouldn't let go of Drey's hand, which made for a rather comical kind of pacing.

And then he began to speak.

Tristol made sure his words were in galactic standard, even though he directed them like harsh clashing colors at the other three galoi. Drey needed to understand almost as much as they did. Perhaps more so.

"I *was* him. My ears are naked and I am nothing." Tristol found himself repeating the ritual words as if they had new meaning, as if they were fresh, as if it were yesterday.

"I am *nothing*. My doctor agreed, my advocate was chosen, my affairs were put in order, and I left. Everyone always thinks exile is a burden. Because other galoi do not feel the pressure to leave. Because they are not strong enough to abandon identity. But Drey, there is so much peace here."

Tris stroked his own naked ears, the outer rim of one and then the other. "There is so much peace in being *zyga*. All Ooloi Villisol wanted was that peace and it was *taken* from him. It was stolen! The only other peace for him then, was the peace of death. Why do you think they let us leave the planet, Drey? The government does not want to let a single *loga* go – not *loga*! Not breeders. But they do. They *always* let us go. They let us go despite being fertile, capable *loga*. We are the hope of all Gal, the last genders. *Yet they let us leave.*"

Drey was still and solid, holding his hand, being a comfort even as he processed Tristol's words. "You're saying that if they didn't let the *loga* become *zyga*, the *loga* would commit suicide? This has happened before?"

Tris did not *know* that. He had not read of it. He had not learned of it, but it *must* be true. Of course the government would not want that information to get out, but it would explain why they were so comfortable letting *zyga* leave the planet. It must have happened before. If a *loga's* whole function, whole existence, was to carry young, yet they knew, deep down, really *knew* that they did not want them? For a *loga* denied *zyga,* there would be only *fear*horror*trappedtrappedtrapped*!

Tris looked up into Drey's kind, human eyes. He wondered at his own capacity to change, that he found Drey's eyes more beautiful with their dark fringed lashes than the purple of his own species. "Drey, *somate*, I would have taken that escape if it was my only option. I was driven to deny everything so that I could leave. Reject my very nature – what society, culture, biology told me I was called into existence to provide."

Drey still looked worried. The wrinkles were in his forehead, a sure sign of distress.

Tris tried another approach. "I read about something once, in your history of human psychology. Claustrophobia. The fear of small places. Humans bred it out or genetic Tinkers fixed it or somehow you left it behind because in space, humans only have small spaces. It's the irrational sensation of everything closing in. That is what it was like for me to be *loga*. The walls were made of the bodies of my own young and they wanted to smother me."

He pressed, needing Drey to comprehend the depth of *zyga* hopelessness. "Please understand, *somate*, that exile is an awful thing. To have no contact with my people, my food, my language, my culture? Near my home on Gal is a flower that blooms once a year for one hour in the middle of the night. It makes a harmonic resonance that is the most beautiful sound in the galaxy. It is impossible to record and impossible to reproduce. I will never hear that sound again. There is a fruit my people sear over open flame that is all flavors all at once – sweet and savory and bitter and salty and so unbelievably tasty. "

Tris knew that his words were now desperate. He didn't care if the galoi understood, but Drey must. "Yet I gave it up. Do you understand? *I gave it all up.* Because even the beautiful parts wanted too much from me, or I wanted too much from them, because to be exile is also to be completely free. Those of us who leave do so because we *must*. It is not a whim. It is survival."

He paused then, swallowed, hunting for the right words, alien words, harsh in his throat. "So yes, I have no doubt that he killed himself."

"And you," Tris looked to the other galoi in the room, remembering that they existed. "You should take those earrings off him, cut his hair, and give his body into space as he deserves. You owe him exile, even if it is only at the last." Oh, how Tris wished that Ooloi Villisol had had an advocate, but he was robbed of even that.

The doctor was the only one brave enough to speak. "But that is cruel."

"To him, no. That it is peace." Tristol's hair spiked in anger at this *isoga*. Her ignorance and manipulation had cost them all so much. Willfully, she had misunderstood, convinced that she knew best.

He wanted her to hurt. He wanted her to feel at least some of what she had wrought. She would receive no punishment for her sins. She had acted in ignorance, relying on *isoga* instinct to protect. Those instincts had simply been horribly misplaced. Galoi did not punish for ignorance. She did not know *zyga* truth. But for Tristol, who had lived too long among humans, that was no excuse.

So he set before her the greatest sin an *isoga* could commit. "Belloi Rissib, you gambled for a life and lost two instead. You forgot what it truly means to be *isoga*. You forgot compassion."

Belloi Rissib's hair wilted.

Drey ran one big human hand through Tristol's angry strands. "Enough, baby."

Tris calmed.

He stared at the three galoi. Purple faces and sad hair. Ignorance that he could only fix by continuing on the path he had already taken, away from them forever. His words here were useless.

Suddenly they did not matter. The past could not be changed. Ooloi Villisol was dead. Perhaps they had learned a little of what it meant to be *zyga*. Perhaps they would not make the same mistake, should a desperate *loga* cross their paths again. But Tristol no longer cared about them.

He wanted to leave this too-big nest. This too-dim spaceship.

He wanted his human space station with its too-bright lights.

He wanted his human lover, with his too-rough skin.

He wanted his own small nest, his own melding of strange and familiar. Peace and exile and home.

"*Somate*," he said to Drey, because identity was important and he refused to be ashamed of what he was and who he loved, "may we leave now? You have solved your murder and found out that it is no murder at all, only mistakes and sadness."

"Yeah, baby, we can leave."

Drey hated this kind of resolution to an investigation.

He'd rather it were a murder in truth. He'd rather there were some real evil for him to catch and collar and punish.

That was so very rarely the case, though. Usually, murder was passion and mistakes and suffering and regret. But this, this was so much worse.

That beautiful mauve man had never needed to die at all.

It reminded Drey of Hu-Core stories. Of the very early days of the sexual awakening. When teens, confused by questions of gender or sexuality or desire, had seen suicide as their only solution. Such a waste brought on by such a profound failure in human culture. Here the galoi too had failed to save one of their own. They had not understood and they had forced the boy to conform to their expectations. So he had taken what he thought was the only way out.

Drey wanted to go hide in Tristol's comforting living room, curl up in the nest that was now theirs, and simply hold his lover close.

Tristol had been so strong. So angry. So empathic. And Tris had managed to escape that fate. He'd known what he needed and seized it with both hands and hair, and wrapped the identity of rejection around himself in a protective shell. Then he'd shot himself into space like a lavender rocket, and landed, rather amazingly, in Drey's cat-scratched arms. He was remarkable.

And if Tris needed to fly away again, Drey would follow him. And if he needed to be let go, Drey would let him, and be grateful for any time that they had had together.

But Tristol was calling him *somate*. Drey knew that was important.

Drey thought from what Tris had said that connection was also part of *zyga*. That Tris was learning and growing and finding his peace through linking to other species not his own. Tris would stay with him and would not be trapped because that was the point. To exile and then share. To leave and then change and expand toward loving others. Drey thought that was why it had to be *loga* who left the planet. Because if they were all like Tris, then they loved easily and openly.

And Tris had chosen to love Drey. And probably Mister Montiguous. And maybe even Mistress Zing and certainly her ramen.

They'd not yet moved to leave. The galoi were still staring at them. But Tris was in his arms and Drey said, "What would you like for dinner tonight, baby, more noodles?"

"I want to go shopping, Drey."

"Socks?"

"No, paint. For the walls of my nest. It is time to add your colors."

"Let's go do that then, my love."

"Drey, that is a new endearment!"

"Well, you've started using *somate*."

"Would you like to know the equivalent human word?"

Drey chuckled, ignoring the wounded curious eyes of the other galoi. "I would."

"*Husband* is almost perfect," said Tris.

"Oh, I see. So by using *somate* you have us married already, do you?"

"Yes, Drey, is that bad?"

"No, baby. But will you conduct the human commitment ritual of spousal contract binding with me first, so that I can call you *husband* by our legal standards?"

"I have been to one of those. It is called a *wedding*!"

"So you know what I'm talking about, then?"

"Drey, you want *a wedding*? With me?" Tris bounced a bit in Drey's arms. The sleeves of Drey's jacket rode up and he noticed, out of context, that his scratches had almost healed.

"Yeah, baby."

"I will get to decorate a human ritual gathering space! May I choose *all* the colors?"

"Yeah, baby."

"Then we will need a great deal more paint, Drey. And after the decorating and the ritual, you will call me *husband*?"

"I will call you *somate* if you wish."

"I would like that, Drey. I would like that very much." Tris pressed his smooth face to Drey's rough beard, a caress of permanence and intimacy, and Drey couldn't believe his good fortune.

Tristol had almost forgotten where they were.

Still on the galoi ship.

Still in the common nest.

Drey took his hand and led him toward the exit. Tris waved his hand in the air at the correct spot and the door telescoped open. They walked through together and back down the hallway of the galoi spaceship, the *sillovin* flowers lethal and beautiful above them. Somehow Tris could like them again. In their way, they had given Ooloi Villisol the exile that he so desperately craved.

Tris did not know or care if the three galoi followed them. They were not important anymore.

But he was stopped at the top of the ramp by a cool hand on his arm. Tristol was so surprised, he jerked. The touch of another galoi.

Drey noticed and paused as well.

Together they turned.

Anisoi Ureeya stood before them.

His *isoga* spouse was there, protective as always, but a little apart, observing from a distance, guarding against intrusion rather than threat.

Tris was confused. He should be back to being invisible – unseen, untouched, nothing.

Yet Anisoi Ureeya's hand still rested on Tristol's arm. Tris was being *touched* by one of his own species. Tris had not had that in so long – the cool softness of another galoi's skin. He had not known he missed it until this moment. But it also itched, bothered him.

It was not warm enough. It felt alien.

"*Zyga?*"

"Yes, *antiga?*"

Anisoi Ureeya let him go, once he was certain he had Tristol's full attention.

Tris allowed his hair to stroke over the spot on his arm,

sooth away the lingering coolness. He squeezed Drey's big, warm hand. His human *somate* was patient, waiting.

The *antiga* stayed silent for a long moment, eyes fixed on where Drey and Tristol's hands were entwined. Fingers woven together like strands of hair, dark brown and lavender. Contrasting but not ugly.

Finally he said, "Tristol, *zyga*, your hair is all one color. Do you have an advocate of record?"

Tris trilled sadly. "I did. The strand went flat and fell out, so I assume that she died." That had hurt more than he would have thought. Not physically. He'd simply awoken one morning to find that one special strand of hair lying flat and lifeless in his nest. He had known immediately that Ooloi Plesol was dead. His last friend. His last true connection to Gal.

Tris pressed on with his explanation. "I was never sent another one. I have been waiting for a new strand for three years now. I thought maybe Gal forgot about me."

"We ignore *zyga* but we never forget them. There are one hundred and three of you off planet right now. And every *zyga* carries the strand of an advocate. Perhaps they were just waiting to find you a younger advocate, for the safety of time."

Tris realized then, that despite *mycota*, despite being captain of a spaceship, despite completing *gamein*, Anisoi Ureeya was quite young himself. Younger than Tris.

"Wait. You are *speaking* to me, anisoi. Why?"

"It is allowed in this instance."

"Oh. You are offering me advocacy? I… Oh, I…" Words would not come to Tris. His hair drifted *sad*hopeful*waiting*.

Anisoi Ureeya switched to galoi and spoke the formal words of binding.

"I Anisoi Ureeya *galoi*male*first gender*complete* would be honored to be your advocate of record Ooloi Tristol *galoi*male*fifth gender*incomplete*."

Tristol's old title and identity. For a brief moment his existence as a true galoi was reestablished. In this one instance Tris *must* be seen completely by another galoi, so that at the very end, when he died, he would be remembered.

Tris recalled the ritual response as if it were yesterday. "I, Ooloi Tristol *galoi*male*fifth gender*completion-irrelevant* accept your sacrifice, Anisoi Ureeya *galoi*male*first gender*complete*."

Anisoi Ureeya, wincing but brave, reached into his own beautiful violet-colored hair and yanked out a single strand. A valuable one, too – long, dark purple, soft, and beautiful.

Drey gasped and said *brash*loud*human*, "What the hell are you doing?"

Poor human, he understood so little.

Tris switched to galactic standard. "All is well, Drey. This is important. Give me another moment, please, *somate*?"

"Of course, baby." Drey subsided, trusting.

*I love this big human,* Tris thought.

Tristol took the offered strand of hair reverently and planted it among his own, feeling it nudge in, take hold, knowing the dark violet color was threading a little with lavender, melding. It would always be different from the others, a single streak of a dark violet. He'd been so vain when he chose Ooloi Plesol as his advocate. He'd wanted her partly because she had his same color hair. Perhaps that was his mistake. She had been too old, so he had outlived her *and* her hair.

Anisoi Ureeya said, "I acknowledged that you are Ooloi Tristol *galoi*male*fifth-gender* no longer."

Tris touched his new strand of hair. "*Zyga*," he agreed. "My ears are naked and I am nothing." Which completed the ritual.

By rights Tris should be invisible again, no longer a person, but Anisoi Ureeya surprised him one final time.

Still in galoi he said, "I look forward to learning the story of your life and singing it to others. Your death will bring great change, I think. And we need that now more than ever."

"Hopefully, not too soon," said Tris, his hair tips flicking in amusement, even the dark purple one.

Tris thought he caught a bit of tip-twitching from the captain's hair too, even though Anisoi Ureeya was back to ignoring him, as was right and proper.

Tristol turned and, tugging Drey by the hand for a change, dragged his frowning, worried human off the alien spaceship.

They stood at the bottom of the ramp a long moment, in the strange, relative safety of the isolated docking bay. They knew that Professor Frills and possibly others were on the other side of the bulkhead, waiting to ask too many questions.

"Tris, did he just give you *a strand of his hair*?"

Poor human *somate*, he was so very confused. "Yes, Drey."

Tristol's emotions were all over the place, and so was the hair in question. It was so unexpected and so very kind of the *antiga*. Tris did not know *antigas* could be kind.

"Anisoi Ureeya is now my advocate of record. I am touched and honored. I lost my first advocate a few years ago. I thought Gal forgot about me. So I would be forgotten utterly too. Now I will be remembered."

Drey noticed the perturbed state of Tristol's hair and gathered Tris close. Soothing him with alien warmth. Tristol loved that already Drey knew what to look for, how to read and understand him, and how to comfort. He was such a wonderful *somate*.

Drey's big human hands nested easily into the coiling lavender strands, occasional petting the darker violet-colored one.

"The strand he gave you has threads of lavender in it."

"Of course, yes. It is mine for the rest of my life."

"What happens then?"

"When I die, my strands will collapse, as Ooloi Villisol's did. All of them will go flat and lifeless, except for that one. That one will stay vibrant and whole, dark violet and lavender together."

"And?"

"And the galoi will know to whom the strand belongs. Our hair color is unique, like human fingerprints. There is a legal mandate governing all *zyga* living among humans. Our bodies *must* be given back to the home world. They must! It is for the hair. You must make absolutely certain, Drey, that my hair is sent home."

"Baby, I think you'll live longer than me. I hope you will. And I'd rather go first."

Tristol nodded. It was a fair request and he would do his best.

"So what happens with that one leftover strand?"

"It is returned to Anisoi Ureeya, as my advocate."

"And?"

"He will tell the galoi my story. My life away from them. And they will know what I have learned of sock shopping and noodle eating and cat keeping. And they will wonder at the differences in our universe. And because of you, they will see that there can be human *somates*, and human love and purple penises, and they will maybe talk a little more to humans. They will maybe open up their ships to visitors. And they will maybe consult your doctors for the secrets of human fertility. And they will maybe *change*. Because that is what *zyga* is for, in the end. Possibility."

Drey was crying, which Tris found odd, but suspected it had something to do with him talking about death, which humans went funny over. As they were funny about all kinds of things.

"Tris, are you saying that galoi hair contains collective memory?" Drey's voice was shaking.

"Of course it does, Drey. Does not human hair?"

Drey gave a watery chuckle and ran a hand over his closely shorn tight black locks. "No, baby. But if it falls to me, I will do everything in my power to ensure your hair makes it back to Gal."

"Good, Drey. I have learned very important things. They should not be wasted or lost."

"Especially not the parts about noodles and purple penises?"

"*Especially* not those."

Drey kissed him and held him a little longer, and then said, "Shall we face the music?"

"There will be music waiting for us in the hallway? Professor Frills plays an instrument?"

"Well he *is* a windbag. But that was an idiom, Tris. Once we've danced to his metaphorical tune, we get to go home to your nest."

"After we purchase brown paint so I may paint you into my life."

"After that, *somate*."

Tristol's hair shivered with joy and he trilled a little at a future with Drey filled with so many new colors and new possibilities – brown and violet and lavender and beautiful.

# GLOSSARY OF ALIEN TERMS

Anisoi: the honorific for an *antiga* galoi, 1st Gender.

*antiga*: connecting (social) and inseminating (physical) galoi, 1st gender, who produce sperm and inseminate eggs. They show human-male-like biological sexual characteristics, but occupy a matriarchal social role. Their skeletal structure is smaller than *isoga* but larger than *loga*. Their skin comes in darker purple colors. They are addressed with the honorific "Anisoi" and their names end in "a" sound. Other galoi who like to bond with 1st gender wear a BLACK earring.

Belloi: the honorific for an *isoga* galoi, 2nd and 3rd gender.

*cota*: the galoi ideal social/sexual adult relationship and cohabitation unit made up of four individuals – one *antiga*, one *loga*, and both *isoga*.

dorien: an alien race that has three genders – male, female, and neutral (or flexible). All three appear to humans as entirely androgynous. Dorien neutral pronouns are xe and xer and are in common use in galactic standard for anyone, regardless of race, who does not identify as male/female. It is also considered polite to address someone as such, if they have not stated a preferred pronoun. Dorien have silver, gray, or white hair (or any combination) and textured skin that looks/feels like an indented tattoo pattern. They are genetically compatible with, and often sexually interested in, humans.

galoi: a xenophobic alien race with 5 genders both socially and biologically based, and a complex. extremely strict biologically-deterministic culture. The planet Gal and its bio-formed galoi were once referred to by the Tinkers as the "platypus of the galaxy." Galoi is both singular and plural (one is a galoi, but also a group of galoi) and also the name of the language.

*gamein*: *a priori* legal social obligation of galoi *antiga* and *loga* to the greater society and culture. It translates to mandated sexual liaisons, for the purposes of procreation, between *antiga* and *loga,* resulting in a required number of viable offspring.

*isoga* (female): protecting (social) and child-rearing (physical) galoi 2nd gender. They have a marsupial pouch (for the joey) and milk-producing teats (like kangaroo), plus residual secondary biological sex characteristics of a female. They don't produce eggs, only milk. They have the largest skeletal structure and skin on the pink end of the purple spectrum. They are addressed with honorific "Belloi" and their names end in "b" sound. Other galoi who like to bond with 2nd gender wear a COPPER earring.

*isoga* (male): protecting (social) and child-rearing (physical) galoi 3rd gender. They have a marsupial pouch (for the joey) and milk-producing teats (like kangaroo), plus the residual secondary biological sex characteristics of a male. They orgasm but they don't produce sperm. They have the largest skeletal structure of all galoi and pinker tones to their purple skin. They are addressed with honorific "Belloi" and their names end in "b" sound. Other galoi who like to bond with 3rd gender wear a GOLD earring.

*loga* (female): nesting (social) and childbearing (physical) galoi 4th gender. They have eggs and a very small womb, plus the residual secondary biological sex characteristics of a female, but they don't produce milk. They have the smallest skeletal structure and come in lighter purple colors. They are addressed with honorific "Ooloi" and their names end in an "l" sound. Other galoi who like to bond with 4th gender wear a SILVER earring.

*loga* (male): nesting (social) and childbearing (physical) galoi 5th gender. They have eggs and a very small womb, but the residual secondary biological sex characteristics of a male. While they orgasm, they don't produce sperm. They have the smallest skeletal structure and come in lighter purple colors. They are addressed with honorific "Ooloi" and their names end in an "l" sound. Other galoi who like to bond with 5th gender wear a WHITE earring.

*mycota*: any sexual/social bonded galoi cohabitation unit from pair to triad comprised of any (culturally acceptable) gender combination. This is considered less desirable and less stable than a full *cota* of four, but it is fine as far as the government is concerned. *Mycota* might loosely be translated as marriage.

Ooloi: the honorific for a *loga* galoi, 4th and 5th gender.

*somate*: a person with whom a galoi forms a working sexual and social bond, similar to spouse.

*zyga*: genderless exiles (by social construct of galoi society), similar to the ancient idea of outcaste. The word "Zyga" is also taken as a last name by galoi *zyga*, and no honorific is used.

# AUTHOR'S NOTE

Thank you so much for picking up *The 5th Gender*. I hope you enjoyed Tristol and Drey's story. If you would like more from the Tinkered Stars universe, please say so in a review. I'm grateful for the time you take to do so.

I have a silly gossipy newsletter called The Chirrup. I promise: no spam no fowl. (Well, maybe a little fowl and the occasional giveaway.)

## *gailcarriger.com*

# ABOUT THE WRITERBEAST

New York Times bestselling author Gail Carriger writes to cope with being raised in obscurity by an expatriate Brit and an incurable curmudgeon. She escaped small-town life and inadvertently acquired several degrees in higher learning, a fondness for cephalopods, and a chronic tea habit. She then traveled the historic cities of Europe, subsisting entirely on biscuits secreted in her handbag. She resides in the Colonies, surrounded by fantastic shoes, where she insists on tea imported from London.

Made in the USA
Las Vegas, NV
15 March 2024

87280075R00132